Garret Logan had [...] open and close

It was early for the onslaught from the usual after-work crowd. He finished drawing ale for the second of two salesmen at the bar before he turned to check on the new arrival. When he did turn, the glass slipped from his hand. He tried blinking away the too-real apparition of a woman he thought was dead. He'd assumed Colleen Drake lay buried in some far-off East Coast cemetery, along with her father, Joe. And with her, a secret the two of them had never told a soul.

Unable to tear his eyes away from the mirage, he said shakily, "Colleen? My God, come closer. Let me look at you." Garret's brain told him he should fill another glass for his waiting customer. At the very least he needed to fetch a mop from the kitchen and clean up this mess. But his boots seemed welded to the worn plank floor as his eyes drank in Colleen's beautiful features.

She stared at him, her eyebrows drawn together.

"You're the second person in this town to mistake me for Colleen. Who is she? Who are you?"

Dear Reader,

I have long been fascinated by the inner workings of a person's mind. Shortly before I proposed this idea to my editor, I had read a magazine article about a young woman who had lost her parents, and suddenly realized that, as an only child, she was the sole keeper of her family history. And as she'd been quite young when her parents died, her knowledge of the history was vague.

This started me thinking about victims of amnesia. People at the mercy of others for their life histories. And so the idea for this story was born, about an amnesia victim who accidentally discovers that much of what she thought she knew about her past is false.

This story is about a young concert violinist who travels to a state she doesn't remember on a journey into a murky past. There she meets a man who loved her, but who has mourned her supposed death for seven years. What transpires is the woman's struggle to find the missing pieces of her life and reach a point where she feels able to accept that she's worthy of love. I hope you enjoy taking the journey with her.

Sincerely,

Roz Denny Fox

P.S. I love to hear from readers, either by e-mail at rdfox@cox.net or by mail at P.O. Box 17480-101, Tucson, AZ 85731.

MORE THAN A MEMORY
Roz Denny Fox

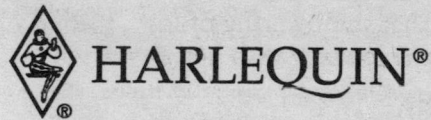

HARLEQUIN®

TORONTO • NEW YORK • LONDON
AMSTERDAM • PARIS • SYDNEY • HAMBURG
STOCKHOLM • ATHENS • TOKYO • MILAN • MADRID
PRAGUE • WARSAW • BUDAPEST • AUCKLAND

ISBN-13: 978-0-373-71509-1
ISBN-10: 0-373-71509-9

MORE THAN A MEMORY

ABOUT THE AUTHOR

Roz Denny Fox has been a RITA® Award finalist and has placed in a number of other contests; her books have also appeared on the Waldenbooks bestseller list. She's happy to have received her twenty-five-book pin with Harlequin Books and would one day love to get the pin for fifty books. Roz currently resides in Tucson, Arizona, with her husband, Denny. They have two daughters.

Books by Roz Denny Fox

HARLEQUIN SUPERROMANCE
1184–A COWBOY AT HEART
1220–DADDY'S LITTLE MATCHMAKER
1254–SHE WALKS THE LINE
1290–A MOM FOR MATTHEW
1320–MORE TO TEXAS THAN COWBOYS
1368–ANGELS OF THE BIG SKY
1388–ON ANGEL WINGS
1412–REAL COWBOYS
1459–LOOKING FOR SOPHIE

HARLEQUIN AMERICAN ROMANCE
1036–TOO MANY BROTHERS
1087–THE SECRET WEDDING DRESS
1185–THE PERFECT TREE
  "Noelle and the Wise Man"

HARLEQUIN SIGNATURE SAGA
COFFEE IN THE MORNING
HOT CHOCOLATE ON A COLD DAY

HARLEQUIN EVERLASTING LOVE
13–A SECRET TO TELL YOU

CHAPTER ONE

JO CARROLL TAPED UP the last of her moving boxes and set it by the door. Only her mother's room remained for her to deal with. Jo had put it off until last. It didn't seem possible that a month had passed since Sharon Drake had been laid to rest next to Jo's dad, Joseph, in the cemetery not far from the apartment she and Jo had shared. Sharon's death had been as unexpected as the car-train accident that had claimed Joe Drake's life seven years earlier.

One morning Sharon woke up complaining of a bad headache. In the blink of an eye she'd collapsed—and was gone before the paramedics arrived. The doctors told Jo it was a brain aneurysm, and she tried to take comfort in the knowledge that her mother hadn't suffered.

Now Jo was on her own. She wasn't a child. At twenty-five she could take care of herself. Since her dad's death, an accident that Jo herself had been lucky to survive, her life had revolved around her career as a concert violinist.

Hesitating at the threshold of her mother's bedroom,

Jo nervously brushed her palms down her denim jeans. Sharon had been an intensely private woman, and a controlling one. Jo had put off this task as long as she could, but she'd crunched the numbers and she knew that moving was an economic necessity. Her monthly stipend as lead violinist with the Boston Philharmonic Orchestra, and the little she earned working odd shifts at a coffeehouse, wouldn't cover the rent on this two-bedroom unit in a renovated brownstone on Commonwealth Avenue.

Her mother had insisted they needed to live where they could rub elbows with symphony patrons who could help advance Jo's career. But Jo wondered how her mom had made ends meet.

Determined to be done with it, she opened an empty box and started sorting her mother's belongings. She set aside a cameo pin to save. Jo planned to donate the rest to a women's shelter. The lack of anything of real value drove home the sacrifices her mother had been willing to make for Jo's profession.

Guilt welled up as she folded a worn, blue crepe dress—the last piece of clothing in the closet. Now, a final check to make sure she'd gotten everything and she'd be ready to call in the movers.

Wait! What was that on the top shelf? Whatever it was had been stuck behind a winter bedspread. She had to stretch, but Jo managed to get down a wooden box. Not too heavy, but it was wedged in tight. Her dad's name was carved on the lid. Jo's hands shook. She had no memories of him. The box was cedar, she realized as she sank to her knees and opened the lid, releasing a pungent scent.

Inside she found books and papers. High-school yearbooks along with news clippings and gilt-edged certificates.

Jo felt momentarily disappointed. She'd been hoping for a will or an insurance policy. But this was strange. The yearbooks were from a high school in Tennessee. White Oak Valley High. Jo didn't know anyone in Tennessee.

As she inspected a couple of the awards, a knot formed in her stomach. The name Colleen Drake was stenciled on each. All were first- and second-place wins from the Smoky Mountain Music Festival.

Breathing became difficult as Jo sifted through two dozen yellowed newspaper articles. A girl pictured in one bore an uncanny resemblance to her own few childhood photographs, which she'd already packed. Here was this Colleen Drake again. A gifted violinist with the same last name as Joe's family.... Fumbling, Jo dropped the clippings. Out slithered a thin gold chain. Hanging from it was some kind of pendant—a gold oak leaf. The leaf was inscribed on the back, Jo saw as she turned it over. Ornate script read *Forever Love*. Under the words were entwined letters that could be a *G* and a *C,* or perhaps two *G*s.

Jo curled her fingers around the pendant. All the items in the box were puzzling. Actually they were a little frightening, she thought, absently tracing a three-inch scar along her hairline. A throbbing pain grew after she opened one yearbook and paged through class photographs. She would've been a high-school sophomore that year. *There was her smile on the face of a stranger named Colleen Drake.* Cold prickles ran up Jo's spine. Her first inclination was to put everything back in the box and pretend she'd never found it.

Curiosity made her open the second book—her junior year. That picture of Colleen Drake resembled her uncannily. It could almost be her—except she never wore her hair pulled back away from her face the way it was in this photo. And Jo's birth name had been Drake, too, until she'd changed it for professional reasons.

The question was unavoidable. Who was Colleen Drake? Could this be *her?* Lights flashed behind Jo's eyes, warning of an impending migraine. She fended it off by sheer will. A cousin—maybe this was a cousin.

A spot in the third yearbook where a graduation photo should have been was blank. But Colleen Drake's name was typed there along with credits listing activities such as track, band and girls' chorus. What had happened to the girl with her face?

Unable to think clearly for the pounding in her skull, Jo cradled her head in her hands. Neatly layered rust-red hair fell forward, veiling the damning evidence.

After a minute, she felt calm enough to begin reviewing what she did know. There wasn't much. The severe injuries she'd sustained in the accident that had killed her father had erased her memory. When she woke up in the hospital following surgery, she'd panicked at her inability to recall anything. But then her mother had appeared at her side. Sharon patiently sat by Jo's bedside and painstakingly reconstructed her past, one story at a time. Some details bubbled up now. According to Sharon, Jo had led a privileged childhood, attending private schools and studying with music tutors. Master violinists. Sharon repeated these stories so often Jo felt as if she remembered living them. Everyone at the hospital considered it a miracle that she'd retained the ability to play her violin. They consulted doctor after doctor who'd all said that sometimes it happened like that following a head trauma. Maybe her memories would return, but maybe they wouldn't.

Why—why would her mother lie to her? Why hadn't she said anything about this cousin or whoever she was? After all, she'd kept these yearbooks.... Fear crept in. Who was left to confirm her mom's accounts of her history?

Scrambling to her feet, Jo found her cell phone and punched in Jerrold Cleary's number with shaking fingers. A longtime patron of Boston's symphony, Jerrold was Jo's mentor and her mother's staunch friend. Jo suspected her mother and Jerrold had a loose romantic relationship, but she had no proof of it, except—

"Jerrold? It's Jo." She broke off her erratic thoughts and found herself babbling. "I thought I'd emptied Mother's closet, but I found a cedar box I think belonged to my dad. This is going to sound bizarre, but…did Mother ever mention me having family? Maybe a cousin, Colleen?" A sigh slid out, but Jerrold's assurance was a relief. He and her mother often huddled together in the kitchen talking while Jo practiced for six or eight hours every day.

"Not that I know of, Jo," Jerrold said. "Are you all right? You aren't making much sense."

"I know. I'm sorry to have bothered you. I'll dig deeper." Jo hastened to say goodbye, but Jerrold cut her off. "You sound funny. I'll be right over."

"There's no need. I'm sure there's a logical explanation for this stuff. This must be a long-lost cousin from Dad's side of the family," she said, trying to believe it. The other possibility was too devastating to consider.

After she'd healed, on a rare outing to a mall, Jo openly envied the young women her age. She'd seen them holding hands and laughing with their handsome boyfriends. Her mother used to hurry her along or divert her attention. Was that significant?

"Don't come over, Jerrold. I'm about to call the movers. I have everything in the apartment packed." *Except for the items from the cedar box.* Jo scowled down at the phone gone dead in her hand.

She didn't call the movers, but returned to her

mother's bedroom and sat down to read the news clippings.

Lost in her reading, Jo felt her heart race when the outer apartment door opened and Jerrold Cleary called her name. She met him in the empty living room. As a rule, his suits were impeccable, and she'd never seen him with a single iron-gray hair out of place. Today he looked rumpled and irritated. "Whatever crap you've unearthed, Jo, it's better tossed out and forgotten."

"Better for whom?" Jo never talked back, and the fact that she did now surprised both her and her visitor. Jerrold waved a dismissive hand.

"Better for your career. Your career is everything. You know your mother devoted her life to ensuring your success. I was going to pop by later with this fantastic news, but I think you need a boost now." Jerrold took a paper from his inner pocket and passed it to Jo. "I've finalized arrangements for you to go on the European circuit this summer," he said, all but preening. "And I negotiated three solos." He wiggled three fingers under Jo's nose, as though she might have misunderstood. "The pieces the conductor wants you to do are listed on the back of the schedule. You've played them all, but you need to start practicing until every note's perfect."

"You aren't listening. What if I'm not alone? What if I have family somewhere?"

He tapped the schedule she hadn't glanced at. "This is a huge coup, Jo. It's just a shame your mother won't get to see you play Ravel's 'Rapsodie Espagnole' on stage in Spain. Hearing you solo on the European circuit was her lifelong dream. But you know that."

Jo had difficulty taking in anything Jerrold was saying. And the ambitious itinerary she held might as well have been written in Chinese. "Jerrold, I can't…go…on this tour."

"Nonsense. I know violinists," he stated in his typically pompous way. "You all get cold feet. But you, Jo Carroll, are the most naturally gifted virtuoso I've ever had the good fortune to mentor. With dedication I predict you'll one day be as famous as Itzhak Perlman or Vladimer Spivakov. And as wealthy," he murmured, straightening his tie. "You, my dear, will be world renowned. My only reward will be to stand in the wings of a sold-out house, watching the audience give *my* protégée standing ovations."

"Jerrold, you aren't getting it." Jo thrust an award certificate at him. "Look at this. I don't know if I'm Jo Carroll. Or am I this other musician, Colleen Drake? It's too much of a coincidence that she looks like me and has the same talent. What if I'm her?"

Jerrold carelessly tore the certificate in half and dropped it. "Jo, you already know you're a Drake. Does the first name really matter? After the accident, Sharon and I decided using her maiden name, Carroll, for your stage name would ensure you privacy. Sharon Carroll would have been famous had she not gotten pregnant with you and been forced to scrap her singing career."

"Mother used to sing around the house." Running a hand through her disheveled hair, Jo circled the nearly empty room. "Daddy made acoustic guitars. And fiddles." She stopped midstride, aghast. "That…all came out of nowhere, Jerrold. *Did* Daddy make guitars? I swear Mother only ever mentioned his violins. Oh, but I could be way off base. Mother auctioned Daddy's wood and his tools on eBay after I was released from the hospital." Jo pressed her aching head to the cool window.

"Stop agonizing, Jo," Jerrold snapped. "It's this move and going through your mother's things. I have no idea why you're insisting on doing this now when you should be spending every minute practicing for the summer tour."

"How can you talk about a tour when my life is in shambles?" Jo wadded up the schedule. She shoved the crumpled ball back at him. "I'm not going to Europe. I mean that, Jerrold. I'm going to follow up on what I've found. It's bad enough that I lost my childhood, but this confusion about what I thought I'd restored…" She raked her hair out of her eyes, this time with a noticeably shaking hand.

"Don't tell me no, you ungrateful little upstart," Jerrold sputtered, his face an alarming shade of red.

At first Jo recoiled from his outburst. But midtirade she yanked open the door. "I'm not a child, Jerrold, so don't treat me like one. I know this is all a huge shock, but something just isn't right."

"Of course," he responded smoothly, plainly making an effort to curb his anger. All trace of irritation left his commercially tanned face as he pasted on a poor copy of his earlier smile.

Paying no attention, she said, "Mother gave you a key to our apartment. May I have it, please?"

"The key? Oh, very well." He handed it over, but only after he straightened the wrinkled tour schedule and pressed it into her free hand. "We'll get together once you've settled into your new studio. The plus side of this move is that it puts you closer to Jordan Hall. When the time comes, after the credits you gain in Europe, you'll be able to audition with the BSO. I'm very close to booking you three hours a week with a master violinist who used to play with the Vienna Philharmonic. He liked the demo tape of your work. I know you'll see this as an example of the great opportunities I can give you."

He sped off, and Jo heard the clatter of his shoes on the stairs before she collected her wits enough to yell, "I'm not changing my mind, Jerrold!" The man ought to realize she couldn't focus on her work when she had question after question tumbling inside her head and no satisfactory answers.

Why wouldn't her mother have told her if they had family in Tennessee? Though she strained to remember, the terrible event remained elusive.

Jo assumed there were gaps in the history her mother rebuilt for her after she'd emerged from the coma. Two neurologists and a psychologist agreed she didn't have retrograde amnesia, but rather dissociative fugue brought on by an intense desire to suppress something she couldn't bear to face. Still, the accident and everything that came before it had been excised from her memory. And yet it made no sense that her mother would've told Jo about her dad's death and not her cousin's—if she'd had one. It was even less likely that Jo would've grown up privileged in Boston, and a sister in some obscure Tennessee town. A place called White Oak Valley. That simply didn't make sense.

Logic told her that something was very wrong. But what if she started digging and found a truth so awful she'd wish it had stayed hidden?

She had pills for these migraines, but it had been a while since she'd needed them. She took one and lay down. When the pain eased she began to reflect on the number of times since the accident she'd felt disoriented—as she did now. The only cure was to immerse herself in music. Her violins were all packed, but she tore the box open. Soon the empty third-floor flat echoed with the rich, haunting sounds of Brahms's "Tragic Overture."

Jo played until her neck got stiff and the fingers of her left hand felt permanently curved around the violin's slender neck. But when she finally set down her bow she knew the uncertainty would suffocate her if she allowed it. Whether it destroyed her career or not, she had to get answers.

LESS THAN A WEEK LATER, after consulting a travel agent, Jo pulled her mother's ten-year-old Subaru off the road in Tennessee at a misty mountain overlook. It had been her original intention to sell the car, but now she was glad she'd kept it. Here she was, less than thirty miles from White Oak Valley.

The bravado that had carried her this far began to falter.

Jo had passed through Sevierville, and Gatlinburg, tourist towns the travel agent had circled on the map. The agent had pointed out that even at the end of May it was still early for the bulk of tourists who flocked to the area for fishing and local crafts.

Resting her arms on a waist-high guardrail, Jo glanced down and was able to identify the silvery thread of a river far below—probably the same one she'd crossed an hour back. The view across the wide valley was partially shrouded by a lavender-gray haze that left Jo oddly breathless. The scene seemed vaguely familiar, as if she'd seen it before—perhaps in a movie or a magazine.

Shivering, she rubbed her upper arms. It was cooler here in the mountains than it had been when she left Boston. Frustrated that nothing had brought back any concrete memories yet, Jo returned to the Subaru, donned a cardigan and drove on to the tiny hamlet of White Oak Valley.

Beautiful full-blooming dogwood trees lined the

main business street that seemed to bisect the small community. Most of these tired buildings had no doubt seen generations of residents come and go: the same families who still lived in the rambling older homes almost hidden by the towering trees.

White Oak Valley lay off the well-traveled tourist highway, and therefore didn't seem to boast the chain restaurants and motels Jo had passed in Gatlinburg. That town's claim to fame was a shrine honoring a TV show, *The Dukes of Hazzard.* Jo had never seen it; her mother always said TV wasted time. So, Jo gassed up the Subaru, but didn't tour Cooter's Place as the young station attendant suggested.

After driving from one end of White Oak Valley to the other, disappointment skidded through Jo. She'd expected something to trigger a breakthrough. Nothing did.

Her stomach growled. It was two hours past her normal lunchtime, and Jo decided to try a café across from the city park—Mildred's, according to a weathered sign. Faded lettering on two plate-glass windows advertised sandwiches, soup, chicken and dumplings, and breakfast at any hour. Jo parked in front of an old-fashioned drugstore and walked back to the café. She pushed open a creaky screen door that released the enticing aroma of home cooking. A 1950s-style soda fountain with chrome-and-red-leather stools ran the length of the room, separating a steamy kitchen from a few tables and vinyl upholstered booths, all of which were empty. Freshly cut sweetpeas sat in fruit jars on every table. Overhead, three white fans would do little to cut the heat billowing from the kitchen once summer arrived.

Choosing a booth near the door, Jo helped herself to a menu tucked behind a remote selector for an ancient jukebox that was even now belting out a country song. She paused a minute and paged through the list of tunes, but realized she'd never heard any of them. Her musical repertoire consisted of symphonies by Beethoven, Schumann, Tchaikovsky and other classical artists.

A pregnant waitress about to pop the buttons off her aqua-blue uniform waddled up. "What can I getcha?" she asked, cracking her gum.

"A bowl of corn chowder and tea," Jo said, thinking that would warm her up. "Anything herbal you have will be fine."

The waitress turned and hollered toward the kitchen. "Mildred, we got any tea back there 'cept the sweet tea Esther made up? We got a customer wanting herbal."

A scrawny older woman, whose age was more apparent because of hair cut short and dyed jet-black, emerged from the kitchen. She took one last puff of her cigarette before crushing the butt in an ashtray next to the cash register.

"We're plumb out of any but Southern sweet tea until I get to the grocery— Well, now." The woman broke off and her jaw sagged even before she collided with the gum-chewing waitress. "Lawdy, if this don't beat all. Everybody thought you was dead, missy."

A shiver wound up Jo's spine, and the menu slipped from her hand. "You know me?" she managed to ask.

At first the woman cackled in disbelief. But as Jo struggled to leave the booth, the woman—Mildred—backed away. "Don't believe in ghosts," she hissed. It was plain she didn't intend to say more.

"Please," Jo implored. "I'm not sure *who* you think I am. I recently discovered some high-school yearbooks from this town. I came here hoping for…I don't know…information, I guess."

"If you ask me, and nobody did, if you *are* Colleen Drake and you ain't dead, you've got some explaining to do. Not to me, but to poor Garret Logan."

"L-Logan?" Jo stumbled over the name. She shook her head to clear her thoughts. "I…my mother never mentioned anyone by that name."

The woman's top lip curled, and she took up a rag to start swabbing the counter. "No surprise there. With her puttin' on airs and thinking you and her were better than anybody born in these parts? May the good Lord forgive me for being blunt, but this town and the Logans will be better off if you trot on back to whatever snooty place you been keeping yourself." Mildred eyed Jo's linen slacks and her matching purse and sandals, then proceeded to shake another cigarette out of a pack of Marlboros she dug out of her apron pocket. Lighting up, she blew a stream of smoke toward the ceiling.

Jo choked on the smoke. Her head began to throb, and she could hardly breathe. This woman couldn't have known her mother if she thought Sharon Drake put on airs. Everything she did was to promote Jo's career.

But it was pointless to argue. Instead, Jo left the café. Making enemies wouldn't get her anywhere. And there was no question but that Mildred thought Jo owed this Garret Logan, whoever he was, an explanation or something.

Perhaps if she tracked him down he could clear up this mystery and she could be back in Gatlinburg before dark, having had a decent meal in a chain restaurant. If that was putting on airs, *she* was guilty of it, not her mother.

Reaching her car, Jo hesitated. She ought to ask Mildred where she could locate Garret Logan.

Fortunately, a boy of about twelve or thirteen passed Jo on a bicycle. He darted her a friendly smile, then swerved toward the city park.

"Hey," she called. "You on the bike. I'm trying to find a man named Logan. Do you know where he is?"

The boy circled back. "Sean just went into the bank."

"Garret. I'm looking for Garret."

"I reckon he'd be at the pub." The boy once again started across the street.

"Thanks, but where's the pub?" The most she got out of the kid was a thumb jerked at the opposite end of the street. She did remember seeing a tavern almost at the edge of town.

She could've walked, but driving gave her a moment to collect herself. She pulled into a graveled lot at the end of a log structure. Jo looked the building over as she locked her car. Neon lettering spilling out of a giant foamy beer mug identified the establishment as Logan's Pub.

At once a different image flashed before Jo's eyes, making her blink. In her mind the sign said not Logan's Pub, but Garret and...someone else's...Pub. The second name swam, refusing to come into focus. The entire image dissipated in an instant. But it lasted long enough to startle Jo, and her sweaty hand slipped off the heavy oak door.

A plaque nailed at eye level announced live bluegrass music on Friday and Saturday nights. Thankfully that sign didn't float or change. Still, her stomach fluttered as Jo stepped inside and took a minute to let her eyes adjust to the dim interior.

Suddenly her knees threatened to buckle as she was overwhelmed by a rush of nostalgia she couldn't explain. A polished bar reflected light from several brewery signs. Her nose wrinkled at the malty smell of beer. As far as she knew, this was the first time she'd ever set foot inside this tavern or any other.

Her eyes skimmed the dark-haired bartender who had his back toward the door as he filled a glass with a dark amber brew. Two other men sat at the farthest end of the bar, deep in conversation. One had a glass of beer and a sandwich in front of him. The other had a sandwich but no beer. Dismissing the men, Jo's eyes lit on a small empty stage opposite the bar.

A loud crash had her whipping her head back toward the bar. The bartender had dropped the glass, and a million winking pieces swam across the floor in a river of ale.

GARRET LOGAN HAD HEARD the front door open and close. It was early for the onslaught of the usual after-work crowd. He finished drawing an ale for the second of two salesmen at the bar before he turned to check on the new customer. When he did, the glass slipped from his hand. He blinked hard, trying to erase the too-real apparition of a woman he'd thought dead for the past seven years. He'd assumed Colleen Drake lay buried in some East-Coast cemetery, along with her father, Joe. And with her, a secret the two of them had never told a soul.

Unable to tear his eyes from the mirage, he whispered a shaky "Colleen? My God, come closer. Let me look at you." Garret's brain said he should fill another glass for the waiting salesman. At the very least he needed to clean up the mess. But his boots seemed welded to the worn plank floor as his eyes drank in Colleen's beautiful features.

She stared at him, her eyebrows drawn together.

"You're the second person in this town to call me Colleen. Who are you? Do you know me?"

No. She couldn't be serious. Garret would know Colleen anywhere in spite of the inevitable changes in her appearance—such as the salon-tamed hair that used to curl wildly around his hands each time he tilted her face up for a kiss. This classy woman who gazed at him from several feet away had a degree of sophistication Colleen had lacked. But it could be no one else. Dammit, half his life had been entwined with hers. He'd loved her even longer than that. Loved her with all his heart. And for seven years he'd grieved over her death. It was only in the past year that he'd been able to consider going on without her. It didn't matter that his large, loving family and host of friends urged him to get on with his life almost daily. Garret's pain at losing Colleen had been too great. They'd planned to be married as soon as he returned from Ireland.

From deep inside a fog of shock, he watched her come closer. In the same smoky voice he'd never forgotten, she murmured, "May I call someone? Did you cut yourself on the glass?"

The formality of her query shook Garret out of his paralysis. The paralysis was replaced by unreasonable anger. He planted both hands on the bar to steady himself. "Where did you run off to? Why are you back now? What do you want from me?"

A dozen questions swirled in her head, but what came out surprised Jo. "If you don't mind, I'll take a sarsaparilla." Truthfully, she had no idea what she had just requested, other than she thought it was some type of soft drink. She hadn't ever tasted sarsaparilla. *Had she?*

Garret didn't smile but said through clenched teeth, "Why don't you and I step outside?"

"Why?" Jo's voice wobbled.

"Because we have an old score to settle."

"What old score?"

"As if you don't know. Give me a minute. I'll get Brian to take over for me here." Abruptly he turned his back on her, grabbed a mug, filled it to the brim and deposited it in front of his customer, who along with his friend was taking everything in. Too shaken to stay in her presence a moment longer, Garret stiff-armed his way through a door marked Private at the back of the bar.

"Who are you? And who's Brian?" she asked, raising her voice.

The door swung shut behind him on silent hinges, leaving Jo gaping at the rude man who hadn't felt the need to share his name.

CHAPTER TWO

GARRET SHOVED THE DOOR OPEN so forcefully he nearly hit his brother Brian, who was toting two trays of clean glasses into the main bar. "Whoa, dude!" His brother jumped aside in the nick of time. "What's your rush?" Only Brian's agility saved them from having to clean up even more broken glass.

"She's back. She's out there." Garret jerked a thumb at the still-swinging door.

"Who? Are you all right?"

"Colleen. Colleen Drake is back. She sashayed right up to the bar, cool as you please, asking for sarsaparilla like she used to. Remember how Mom stocked sarsaparilla at home for her? And Dad had it here because it was all Colleen liked, but her mother nixed soda pop. Sharon said sugar made Colleen too high-strung to play her violin."

"Slow down. You're babbling, my man. Take a deep breath. Colleen's been dead for seven years. You've probably gone and scared off a customer, Garret." Brian set the heavy trays on the kitchen island that held a six-burner stove and a well-used grill.

Garret was ready to yell at his older brother, but with a backward glance at the door, kept his voice low. "It's her, I tell you." It was true he hadn't set eyes on Colleen Drake since her whole family left town while he escorted his mother to Ireland for her family reunion. But Harvey Bolton, the real estate agent who sold the Drakes' house, told everyone Joe and Colleen had died in a car accident.

Brian laid a hand on Garret's shoulder. "Garret, maybe you should go home and let me handle the bar. Sean showed you the newspaper article about the accident. You must be mistaken. They say we all have a twin somewhere in the world."

"Right, and Colleen's twin happens to love sarsaparilla? I'm telling you, Brian, it's her." Garret shook off his brother's hand. "I can't deal with her right now. Do me a favor. Ask her how long she's going to be in town and where I can find her when I calm down some." Garret's voice cracked. Elbowing his brother aside, he pulled a set of keys from his jeans pocket. "Sorry to leave you shorthanded. Oh, yeah—I dropped a full glass of Sam Adams. There's glass and beer all over behind the bar." He hesitated, as if wanting to say more, but instead, yanked open the pantry and hauled out a fifth of Bushmills Irish whiskey, then left by the back door.

Brian Logan chased after his brother. "On second thought, Garret, if you're right and it is Colleen Drake, I probably won't be very nice to her. How could I after what you've been through? Give me the whiskey. Go back and talk to her yourself. Don't let that woman drive you back into the bottle."

"I won't. I need a little liquid courage, is all, before I tell her exactly what I think." Garret wagged the bottle.

"Dammit, you've been back to your old self this year."

Garret didn't respond. He brushed past Sean, his brother closest in age, who was returning from a run to the bank. Along with Garret and Brian, Sean was part-owner of the pub.

Without a word to Sean, Garret climbed into his Suzuki Grand Vitara and sent up a spray of gravel as he tore out of the lot.

"What's got his tail in a twist?" Sean gestured with an empty bank deposit bag toward the rapidly receding vehicle.

Brian took the bag from Sean. "I need to attend to business inside. Go after Garret. Make sure he's okay. He's just had the shock of his life. I'm guessing he's headed to his house."

"What kind of shock?"

Brian glared angrily back at the pub. "I haven't seen her yet, but apparently, Colleen Drake has returned from the dead. From hell, if you ask me, considering the basket case she left Garret."

"But…we all saw the news photo of Joe Drake's car being loaded onto a flatbed truck. The article said the driver and passenger were pronounced dead at the scene. There's no way anyone could have survived that wreck."

"Yeah, well, either Garret's suddenly lost his mind, or the reporter got his facts wrong. Go. Make sure Garret doesn't polish off too much of that bottle. And if he's too rattled to come back and handle the after-work crowd, see if Molly can come in," Brian instructed, referring to their only sister.

Sean struck out for his pickup. "I'll phone Mom. Then Trish and Jaclyn," he said, looking relieved that Brian would be the one dealing with their surprise visitor.

Brian nodded. "I'll see if I can find out why she's here, and how long she plans to stick around. I wonder where she's staying."

"Not too many choices. Trish is working the desk at the resort this afternoon. When I phone her, I can ask if Colleen checked in. If not, maybe it wouldn't hurt for Trish to tell her they're full up. She might just decide to move on."

"She's Garret's business, Sean, not ours. Maybe she has a good reason for being gone so long."

"What good reason could there be for letting Garret dangle for seven damn years? He bought land to build her a house, for cripe's sake. He deserves an explanation at least, Brian."

"Right. You're right. Our folks always treated Colleen like a second daughter. Like they treat my wife and Galen's and now your fiancée. I can't think of any excuse that's strong enough for us to forgive how badly she hurt Garret. Go, do what you have to, Sean. I'll see if it's really Colleen at the bar, and not some figment of Garret's imagination." Brian returned to the pub's kitchen where he grabbed a broom, bucket and mop and went to tackle his brother's mess.

A FEW TIMES on the drive home Garret considered turning back. Part of him knew Brian was right in saying he'd come a long way this past year. He was also right that Garret shouldn't let Colleen send him into a tailspin again. But he couldn't help it.

There was the note she'd left with his dad shortly after he accompanied his mom on the trip to Ireland. In it she said she was going to Boston with her parents for a few days—strictly to pacify her mother. She said her mom had arranged for an audition at some high-brow music conservatory. But Colleen assured Garret that she had no intention of attending any music school so far away.

Today she'd looked spiffy enough to have become one of the highbrows. What the hell had happened to her resolve?

Garret pulled into his driveway but he didn't get out. He gripped the steering wheel with both hands. A few weeks before Garret, and his mom, Clare, arrived home from three months abroad, the top real estate agent in White Oak Valley sold the Drake house, which sat next to the Logan family homestead. The story that circulated and had been accepted as truth was that Harvey Bolton had been contacted by a grief-stricken Sharon Drake and told to sell. Well, jeez, Garret had been grief stricken, too. And inconsolable, even though his family had banded together to try to ease his pain. Dropping his head briefly on the steering wheel between his two clenched hands, he realized the story could only have been a ruse.

He beat his palms on the wheel and released a strangled cry. Then he grabbed the bottle of Bushmills and made his way into the house he and Colleen had planned together.

JO HAD BEEN SHAKEN by the angry words flung at her by the bartender. She was half-afraid to meet him outside as he suggested. The pub was surrounded by forest. No one except a kid on a bicycle knew she'd come here looking for Garret Logan. How could she trust that surly, muscular bartender not to hurt her?

Still, those people might be her only lead, her only way to sort out the past. She was unnerved by his behavior, but even more so by her own uncharacteristic request for sarsaparilla.

As Jo hovered near the bar, undecided about leaving or staying in case the man came back, she sensed a bigger wall of hostility surrounding a second man who'd emerged from the pub's back room. He carried a broom, a mop and a bucket. After pausing to check if the two guys seated at the bar needed anything else, he bent to the chore of cleaning up the mess left by the first bartender. If this was the Brian the other man had mentioned, he wasn't familiar to her either.

The two men, both quite good-looking with dark hair and coffee-brown eyes, shared a familial resemblance. Plus, they were the rudest people Jo had ever encountered. Her ego still smarted from the first man saying they had a score to settle. The only scores she knew anything about were musical scores.

She supposed she could've explained her situation. She could've admitted her past was a blank. But a psychologist she'd briefly seen had cautioned her to be careful whom she confided in before she knew just how the person was linked to her past. The therapist said sometimes too much honesty allowed unscrupulous people to take advantage. She cited cases where men—especially—had claimed past romantic relationships with fugue victims, then cleaned out their bank accounts. And her mother, too, had urged Jo to be wary because she was so vulnerable.

Not that Jo had money. What she did have, apparently, was some kind of history connecting her to this town. Already she'd experienced the anxiety that accompanied flashes of déjà vu. And, yes, she definitely felt vulnerable. The bartender had also called her Colleen. Jo didn't know what to believe.

Glancing around the pub, she felt as though she'd seen the paintings and photographs hanging on the walls before. It was creepy, like walking into a stranger's dream.

Still unsure if she should wait for the first bartender to return, Jo crossed to a doorway shielded by strings of green crystal beads. She parted the tinkling strands and peered into a vacant room—and was flooded with images of a wedding. Or perhaps bits and pieces of several wedding receptions. The mental pictures were so clear they made her gasp and blink.

She started to step into the room, but was blocked by a man's arm. Jo fought the barrier momentarily, because she didn't want to lose the moment. The blip— the wedding scene—was accompanied by raucous laughter, clinking glassware and the sounds of loud fiddle music.

Not Jo's kind of music—not Tchaikovsky, Schumann or Beethoven—but folk songs. How was it she recognized the bluegrass sounds when her mother refused to let anything other than classical music be played in their home?

Checking her forward motion, Jo dropped her chin and gripped her head. Briefly, she recalled one of her hospital nurses bringing her a CD of country instrumentals. Her mother had pitched a fit and snapped the CD in half. "Trash," Sharon spat, as she tossed the broken pieces in a wastebasket.

"This room is off-limits," the man growled. "Haven't you hurt Garret enough? He's finally getting his life back. I can't control who comes and goes in this town, but it is my call as to who gets served in Logan's." For a brief moment he relaxed his gruff stance. "Forget whatever's brought you back to town, Colleen. Believe me, there's nothing left for you here."

Overcome by unexplained dizziness made worse by the man's intense brown gaze, Jo decided she'd had quite enough Southern hospitality for one day. "I wasn't planning on stealing the family jewels," she said, gritting her teeth. "I came here hoping to speak to Garret Logan. But it's clear you people have never learned basic good manners." Not waiting to see what, if any, effect her outburst had, she turned and stalked off. She couldn't get out of the building fast enough.

Outside in the fresh air it took several minutes to calm her nerves. The odd moment she experienced in the pub could only be a glimpse into her past. Mildred at the café and both bartenders seemed sure they knew her. They called her Colleen, the name in the high-school yearbooks and on the award certificates she'd found in the cedar box. Her father's cedar box.

It was frightening to think about who she might have been. What could she have done to spark such negative reactions?

Jo's inclination was to climb in her car and get out of this burg where it was abundantly clear she wasn't wanted. It would be easy to take Jerrold's advice and leave buried what her mother had taken such pains to hide.

But that would be cowardly. Jo had fought back

from the brink of death, the doctors said. Whatever she was, she wasn't a coward.

And yet her hand shook as she switched on the ignition. Probably because of the second bartender's barely veiled threat that there was nothing for her in White Oak Valley. It was disturbing to think she might have committed a sin here so awful that after a long absence she'd still be persona non grata.

Slowly releasing the brake, Jo cast a final look at the pub before stepping on the gas. Was she crazy for wanting explanations?

No! Anyone who'd ever lived without memories would know it left a person feeling incomplete. Surely it was better to step up and face whatever crime she'd committed as a teenager. All sorts of possibilities chased through Jo's mind, from the simple to the really drastic. Nothing seemed to click.

As she drove aimlessly around town, Jo recalled the past her mother had drilled into her after she'd emerged from the coma. She recalled how panicky she'd felt when no memories would come. No wonder she'd accepted the stories her mother had spun. In pain, recovering from multiple surgeries, why would she question any of it? And the pieces fit, especially after her doctors agreed to let Sharon bring Jo's violin to her bedside. The realization that she remembered how to play had eased her initial panic. She realized now, belatedly, that was the biggest factor as to why she swallowed everything her mother had told her.

Except, how much was fact and how much fiction? The staff at the conservatory welcomed her with open arms after she'd healed enough to attend classes. That year and later, instructors often spoke in glowing terms of her first auditions. And Jerrold had signed on as her sponsor prior to the accident. So her talent, at least, was real.

But when had her parents left White Oak Valley, and why?

That was the million-dollar question Jo needed to answer. And she wasn't going back to Boston until she had. She remembered passing a resort hotel on one of her swings through town. Circling back, Jo was relieved to see only a handful of cars in the lot. Her bank account was healthy enough to allow her to stay a few weeks.

She parked and went inside. To the left of an empty lobby, a dark-haired woman not much older than Jo stood behind the check-in counter. Her badge said Trish Collier.

"I'd like a room, please." Jo smiled as she slid a credit card from her wallet. "Three nights to start. Possibly more. I'm not sure how long my business in White Oak Valley will take."

"Sorry," the clerk said. "We're full up," she added, turning away to sort through a pile of registration slips.

Jo glanced down the two corridors she could see from where she stood. The place was as silent as a tomb.

The clerk noticed and said, "Most of our guests are out on a tour of Smoky Mountain National Park."

"Ah. Then could you recommend another hotel in town? Anyplace clean and safe."

"You won't find any vacancies in the valley. White Oak Valley's Spring Arts and Crafts Fair starts tomorrow. There's nothing from now until the Mountain Music Festival in mid-June. All area hotels and resorts are booked as much as a year in advance."

"I see." Jo returned her credit card to her purse. Her thoughts tumbled back to the award certificates in her car. Was that the same mountain music festival? If so, it would pay off to see if anyone connected to judging the contest remembered her. Jo's experience in the world of music told her the same folks judged year after year. Someone was bound to remember a girl talented enough to win so many contests.

Thanking Trish Collier for her time, Jo left the resort. Possibly she'd have to leave the valley now and come back for the music festival in June. It went without saying that she was hugely disappointed.

Jo decided to take the long route out of town, admiring the scenery on both sides of the country road. That was how she came to spot a bed-and-breakfast with a Vacancy sign blowing gently in the late-after-noon breeze. Jo's heart beat faster. Could she be so lucky?

She quickly made a U-turn and sped back to take a closer look at the two-story home with its wide, appealing veranda. Everything about it, from its butter-yellow paint to Wedgewood-blue shutters, to the American flag fluttering above the broad front steps, looked inviting. A handicap ramp made the wicker porch furniture accessible to any manner of traveler.

Jo pulled in, got out and practically skipped up to the front door. "Hi," she called to a young woman she spotted through the screen. "Is your Vacancy sign for real? I understood most area hotels are booked solid till June."

A slender blond woman opened the screen door. "I wish that was true for us. We have six rooms to rent. You can have your pick." She named a price and said it included breakfast, plus afternoon tea and a homemade snack.

Jo thought that amount was more than reasonable. "Do you take credit cards?" If they operated on a cash-only basis that would be a drawback. She couldn't fathom why else the other accommodations were full and not this charming place.

"We take all major credit cards. By the way, I'm Kendra Rowan. Welcome to Buttercup Cottage." Kendra stepped aside, allowing her guest to enter. "My husband, Jim, and I have spent the better part of two years renovating this house. It belonged to Jim's grandmother. We're originally from California. Jim was an army cook. He, uh, lost both his legs when his convoy was hit by an IED in Iraq." Kendra paused to draw a breath. "That's probably way more than you want to know. Jim always says I tend to ramble. But I wanted to assure you he's still a great cook."

"I'm so sorry," Jo burst out. "You're both to be commended. This place looks fabulous. It had to be a huge undertaking with or without handicaps."

"Our biggest challenge came after Jim's surgery. He'd always dreamed of opening a restaurant one day. After his accident, he lost heart. All the credit goes to the rehab doctors and nurses who convinced him a kitchen could be modified. Jim's so close to realizing his dream, if we can attract more customers like you."

Jo saw Kendra discreetly wipe a tear from her cheek. "Once word gets out, you'll be swamped," Jo said earnestly, handing over her credit card. "Charge three nights. If I decide to stay longer, I'll let you know." Jo was tempted to share her own story with Kendra, but something held her back. Until she found out exactly what her connection was to this town, it might be better not to give Kendra or her husband any reason to mistrust her.

With the paperwork complete, Jo accepted Kendra's suggestion of a second-floor room decorated in cool blues and Victorian furniture. A dormer window overlooked the valley that was again layered with gauzy, bluish fog.

When Jo commented on the mist, her hostess said, "Jim's dad grew up in this house. He told us the Cherokee called this territory Shaconage." She pronounced it sha-con-ah-jey. "The name means 'land of blue smoke.' If this is your first visit to the Great Smoky Mountains, I hope you plan on seeing our many historic sites. I thought it would be hard to leave the bright lights of San Francisco, but in the two years we've been here, I've fallen under the mountains' magic spell. I tell Jim it's like we're living in a fairyland. You'll see what I mean."

Jo surprised herself by saying, "This isn't my first visit to the valley." When it seemed as if Kendra was waiting for her to elaborate, Jo added, "But I was here so long ago everything seems brand-new."

Kendra put down the flowered pillow she'd been plumping. "White Oak Valley seems stuck in slow motion to me. But given the changes we've made to this house, it probably looks a lot different from when you were last here. Well, I'll let you get settled in. If you need anything, just let me know."

"Thanks, but I'll be fine. I may hike into town for dinner and make it an early night. The mountain air has sapped my energy."

Kendra nodded. "If you'd rather not walk to town, Jim can fix you a sandwich. We have lemonade or iced tea. You can eat on the veranda, in the breakfast room or up here. Our hope is that guests will consider Buttercup Cottage a temporary home."

"No need to put your husband out. I know there's a café on Main Street. Is that the extent of places to eat in White Oak Valley?" Jo hoped not. She wasn't looking forward to a second encounter with Mildred.

"There's Logan's Pub, but you'd have to drive there. It's at the opposite end of town from us. They serve steak, chicken and great burgers, which all come with their signature coleslaw and steak fries."

Wasn't that just her luck? "That seems like more food than I had in mind. I think I'll accept your offer of a sandwich and iced tea. I'll bring in my suitcase and then come down and enjoy a peaceful evening on the veranda."

Kendra beamed. "Jim will be thrilled to serve our first customer. Anytime you want breakfast tomorrow, poke your head in the kitchen. Once we get full up we'll set more structured meal times. Until then, we'll operate on a looser schedule. I'll hear if you go out. I'll freshen your towels and make up your room then. Eventually we'll hire staff, but for now it's just us."

"That sounds fine to me." Jo left to collect her things from her car. Two vehicles, a car and a pickup, passed as she retrieved her bag and her violin from the trunk. It seemed to her that both drivers slowed and were staring at her. But maybe she was paranoid. Buttercup Cottage did sit on a sharp curve. It was why she'd slowed for a closer look. *Yep, she was paranoid.*

Kendra met her at the door and held it open for her. "Let me run your things upstairs. Jim said if you'll take a seat at the wicker table, he'll bring a tray right out. Ohh, do you play the fiddle?" Kendra asked excitedly when Jo passed her the case. "Logan's Pub features a bluegrass band on weekends. We go every chance we get."

"I play violin," Jo corrected. "I'm a concert violinist. As a matter of fact, if it won't disturb you, I should do a little practicing. I won't if other guests check in."

"You go right ahead. Practice to your heart's content. Did you notice the piano in the sitting room? Jim plays when I beg him. We want guests to feel free to use it, too. Maybe you guys could knock out a duet while you're here."

Jo smiled, thinking how much more appealing that sounded than Jerrold's proposed solo European tour. In the past her practice schedule hadn't allowed her to cultivate friendships. She almost wished she could stay in White Oak Valley and be friends with Kendra Rowan. Then Jo remembered the stir she'd caused at Logan's Pub. That put a damper on any thoughts of staying.

Jim Rowan wheeled onto the porch through a sliding door Jo hadn't noticed when she sat down. "Kendra didn't ask if you preferred roast beef or a tuna sandwich," he said. "So I made you a half of each."

"I like both. Thank you so much," Jo said, watching him unload the metal tray neatly clamped over the arms of his wheelchair. "It's a lovely place you have here."

"Yeah. There were times I didn't think it would ever come to pass. I'm happy to break in easy with one guest to start. Don't know how you feel about being my guinea pig." He grinned and his white teeth flashed in his freckled face. His sandy hair was still cut military short, giving him a boyish look. In reality he was probably a few years older than Jo's twenty-five, she thought as she joined in his laughter.

"If this is homemade bread, I'll gladly be your guinea pig," she said, taking her first bite.

He appeared more than satisfied with her response, and whistled as he motored off, leaving Jo to eat in solitude. She lingered over a refill of tea, watching fireflies dance above a gurgling creek that flowed past the side of the cottage. When mosquitoes found her, she carried her empty plate and glass into the kitchen. She retreated to her room, where the unfamiliar silence threatened to overwhelm her. Taking Kendra at her word, Jo pulled out her violin and tuned the strings. Her mother said this well-used instrument had been Joe Drake's sixteenth-birthday gift to his daughter. It bothered Jo that she had no recollection of that birthday or any other. No holidays or special events before coming to in the hospital. She'd missed celebrating her nineteenth birthday because she'd been in the coma.

Settling the violin under her chin, Jo tested the bow, tightened it, then plunged into Tchaikovsky's "Serenade for Strings." When life got too complicated, she tended to lose herself in the mellow, flowing sounds. Still, she was shocked to see the bedside clock showing midnight when she stopped playing because of aching wrists. Jo couldn't have named all of the pieces she played after Tchaikovsky's "Serenade." One had blurred into another. However, she felt calmer and knew she would sleep.

The next morning, Kendra glanced up shyly when Jo peered into the kitchen as instructed.

"You play like an angel," Kendra said with awe. "I'm not well versed in chamber music, but I cried listening to you play. You make your violin weep."

She ushered Jo to a table in the dining room set for one. Gleaming white china and polished silver graced snowy linens. A single red rose in a slender bud vase added formality to the setting.

"You should have said you were famous," Kendra went on. "After we heard you play, Jim searched your name on the Internet. Mercy, you let me go on and on about Jim's injury, when you had your own recent tragedy…losing your mother so suddenly."

Jo's stomach tumbled. "Where did you read about me?"

"An article in yesterday's *Boston Globe* had an interview with a patron of the philharmonic orchestra, Jerrold somebody, who called you the best violinist of this decade. He said you're touring with a prestigious European orchestra this summer, but you've taken time off from performing in Boston to grieve for your mother. Shut me up, but *why* White Oak Valley? We're so the back of beyond." Kendra dropped her voice. "Is it a man? Has to be, to make you play such heart-stopping songs. Your music last night sounded sadder than sad."

Her host's fluttering about made Jo nervous. "My coming to Tennessee is nothing so cloak-and-dagger. And I'm not *that* famous," she added dryly.

Jim Rowan motored out of the kitchen. He slid two delicious-looking strawberry crêpes onto Jo's plate. From his tray, he unloaded a small bowl of whipped cream and a steaming pot of tea. "Pay Kendra no mind. My wife has a vivid imagination. She's hooked on romantic suspense novels, so she's always looking for love and intrigue. We'll be in the kitchen if you need anything," he said, pointedly grabbing his wife's hand to drag her away.

Jo let them go before she tucked into the rich breakfast. She could strangle Jerrold. She'd dumped dozens of his calls from her cell last night. Her story was newsworthy and might make a good book, she conceded, but he had no right to speak about her without permission. Kendra would be disappointed that there was no romance involved. Jo'd never had time to cultivate a man's friendship, let alone think of romance.

The front door opened as she sipped her tea. Her seat gave her an unobstructed view of the woman who entered the foyer. She was of medium height and her light brown hair curved artfully around her narrow face. Jo noticed the dour expression, because the woman's hazel eyes narrowed on her. Feeling a bit as if she'd been caught with food on her face, Jo reached for the napkin she'd had draped across the knees of her oldest jeans. Another reason to feel uneasy. The woman studying her like a bug under a microscope was impeccably dressed in heels and a flowery spring dress.

Gripping an envelope purse, the newcomer hurried across the floor until she stood in front of Jo. "So the rumor's true. You are back. There's a lot of speculation as to why, Colleen. I'm happy to see you didn't die, but if you've had second thoughts about dumping Garret, forget it. You had your chance with him, and you screwed up. Now it's my turn. In fact—" she wiggled her left hand "—I intend to be wearing Garret's ring by the end of the arts and crafts fair. We'll be on our honeymoon by the start of the Mountain Music Festival—if that's what's brought you back to the valley."

"What…who…?" Jo was too stunned to do more than croak. A tiny window in her brain cracked open long enough for her to know this wasn't the first time she'd met the brunette. Then the window closed with a snap, leaving Jo gaping after a total stranger. A stranger who departed as quickly as she'd come.

Jo half rose, but the screen door shut before she could get to her feet. She sat again and heard an expulsion of breath that she knew hadn't come from her. Glancing up, Jo saw Kendra and Jim hovering in the kitchen doorway.

"Who…was that?" Jo asked.

"Jaclyn Richmond," Kendra said. "A local artist. She came by the day Jim's dad put up our outdoor sign, asking if we'd display some of her paintings in our rooms. I guess she wanted us to sell them. But her work was too modern for our Victorian decor. Mrs. Applegate at the corner grocery store said Jaclyn used to be married to a football player, but the marriage fell apart. Now I hear she's running after Garret Logan."

"She seemed to know you," Jim said, interrupting Kendra's prattle.

Kendra wasn't done, however. "Why did she call you Colleen? You signed our register as Jo Carroll, and that's the name we used to find you on the Internet."

Sighing, Jo folded her napkin, and decided it was time to trust them. "It's a long story, or a short one, depending on how you view it. I can't answer your question, Kendra." Jo stood up. "I was in an auto accident seven years ago and have holes in my memory. Jaclyn Richmond and others in town may know more about me than I do. I came here hoping to learn about my past. It seems not everyone seems happy to see me."

Kendra slid a hand onto her husband's shoulder and studied their guest with troubled eyes. "If you need friends you can count on Jim and me. This is a very tight community and it can be hard to break in. There are some who consider us outsiders even though Jim's grandparents lived here a long time and his dad was born here."

"Thanks. But I should probably check out and find a room somewhere outside White Oak Valley."

"We want you to stay, don't we, Jim?" Kendra nudged him.

The man in the wheelchair caught and kissed his wife's hand. "Kendra's very stubborn when it comes to getting through tough times. She says stay, and I agree with her."

"I will, then," Jo said. "I appreciate your generosity. I really hope to straighten everything out in a day or two. With your blessing, I'll get right to it."

CHAPTER THREE

ON THE OTHER SIDE of town from the Rowans' B and B, Clare Logan knocked on her son Garret's kitchen door. His dog, Domino, a black-and-white spotted hound, barked and jumped up to bat the glass, but there was no response from Garret. Clare shifted the load she carried and, after a sharp command for the dog to sit, let herself in. "There's a good boy," she murmured as the hound sniffed her shoes, whined, then padded over to his empty food dish and gave her a pathetic look. "I see your master has fallen down on the job this morning. Let me check on him, then I'll get you some kibble."

"Garret," she called again, "it's Mom. I've brought homemade breakfast rolls and black coffee." Clare set the still-warm rolls and the thermos on the granite counter. She tsked over the lack of any sign that Garret had eaten the night before.

Making her way to the living room, she wasn't surprised to find her youngest son passed out on his leather couch, still wearing yesterday's clothes. His left hand was wrapped limply around a half-empty bottle of

Bushmills that rested on the floor. Grimacing, she took away the bottle, capped it and unceremoniously rolled Garret off the couch onto the hardwood floor.

"Cripes," he yelped, coming alive. "Can't a man get peace and quiet in his own home?" He tried levering himself up on both elbows, but groaned and fell back flat. He flung an arm over his eyes to protect them from the bright morning sunlight as his mother threw open his drapes.

"Dad and I heard from all three of your brothers last night. They said you tossed them out of here so you could wallow in self-pity. I was willing to let you mope for one night. Now it's time to buck up and display a little Logan pride."

Clare stowed the whiskey bottle in an otherwise empty portable bar, spun back toward her son and settled her hands on her hips.

"Go away," he groaned. "Can't you all see I just want to be left alone?"

A petite woman whose head barely reached the shoulders of her husband, Donovan, or any of her four sons, Clare Logan was nevertheless no weakling. She proved it now by hooking Garret under his arms and muscling him to his feet. He swayed unsteadily, but with his mother's assistance, managed to stumble toward the downstairs bathroom. "Time for a shower," Clare announced. "You smell worse than the pub after a bachelor party. I'll fetch you some clean clothes, then I'll feed Domino. A chore you should have handled hours ago."

"Jeez, take it easy, okay? My head feels like I got kicked by a mule." Garret leaned both palms on the sink and peered into the mirror before passing a shaky hand over his stubbled jaw. "I'm entitled to tie one on, Ma. Or didn't Brian tell you who showed up at the pub yesterday afternoon?"

Clare crossed her arms, but her expression became a shade more sympathetic. "Sean phoned first, then Brian. Honey, we've all watched you be depressed over that girl for too long. We grieved with you in the beginning. Back then we loved her, too. Now I'm mad as hell. She couldn't have phoned or written to you once in all that time? You know she could have."

Garret's jaw twitched as he gritted his teeth.

"Oh, son, it's been so good this past year to see you getting back to the Garret we all know and love. None of us are willing to stand idly by and let Colleen Drake send you into another black hole."

Garret winced as his mother rolled Colleen's name bitterly off her tongue. "Men don't get depressed," he argued. "I missed her and floundered for a while is all."

"That's the kind of stubborn thinking that kept you from enjoying life. You found out whiskey didn't help before. It won't do anything now."

Garret sagged and his chin hit his chest. "I did try drowning my sorrows in booze. Luckily I hate hang-overs." And after several stiff drinks last night, Garret convinced himself he'd been mistaken yesterday at the pub. Now he wasn't sure. "So," he said, heaving a sigh.

"She's really alive? I started to hope, as Brian suggested, that it was her double."

"Don't we wish? No, she tried to book a room at the resort. Sean figured she'd stop there, and he called Trish to warn her. She made up a story about all the area hotels being full from now through the Mountain Music Festival. Sean and Brian hoped Colleen would leave and go on her merry way. Unfortunately, no one told the Californian couple who opened that new B and B in the south end. Galen was driving home from work and saw Colleen hauling her luggage into the old Rowan house." Galen was the eldest of Clare's four sons, and the only one not involved in Logan's pub.

"Why do you suppose she came back after all this time?" Garret muttered half to himself as he turned on the shower. "At first, I could have sworn she didn't recognize me. Then she hiked herself onto a bar stool and ordered sarsaparilla like she always did. I, uh, yelled at her in front of customers—a couple of salesmen traveling through White Oak Valley who'd stopped in for a beer. I realized what I'd done, and told her to meet me outside. But I just couldn't face her. Seeing her was like an electric shock, Ma."

"I'm disappointed in her. She doesn't seem the least bit fazed by how she treated you, Garret. Brian said he told her she was wasting her time sticking around. This morning Jaclyn paid her a visit. She told Colleen that you and she are dating. I detoured past the B and B on my way here, thinking she'd have taken the hint to go.

I assume it's her car with Massachusetts license plates still parked in their lot."

"Jackie should've stayed out of this. If there's fighting to be done, it's between me and Colleen."

"Jaclyn's seen you at your worst. She cares about you, Garret. You two have more in common than you'll admit. She knows what it's like to have your heart broken."

"Yeah, but even so…"

"This room's steaming up." Clare reached inside the door and turned on the noisy exhaust fan.

Grimacing at the stab of pain in his head, Garret quickly shut the fan off. "Ma, I've told you—told the whole family—I'm simply not in the market for a wife. I wish you'd all listen."

Clare held up a hand. "Take your shower, Garret. Domino's been waiting long enough for his breakfast, so I'll take care of that after I drop some clean jeans and a shirt outside your door. Once you feel yourself again, we can hash this out over coffee and rolls."

"No food, Ma. Coffee, black and plenty of it, will do me. Thanks for sobering me up, but there's nothing to talk about." He meant that, too, as he shut the bathroom door and stripped out of clothes that did smell like swill. Garret loved his family, but at times they could be too interfering.

Stepping under the pelting spray, he tried to force his thoughts to focus. Not that he wanted to revisit the pain he'd suffered in the years after his return from

Ireland. He'd brought home a wedding ring he'd intended to put on Colleen's finger. So many times, he'd imagined how the stones would flash under the pub's stage lighting whenever her talented fingers worked their magic on her fiddle strings. What would his family say if they knew how often, when he was alone, he took out the ring and the fiddle Colleen had played at the pub whenever he could talk her into it? She'd played there in spite of her mother's vehement objection.

There was one thing Garret knew to be true. Sharon Drake had never liked him. She'd chased him back through the hole in the hedge between the Drake and Logan houses too often to count.

Over the years he and Colleen had gotten good at finding ways to steal time together. There'd never been anyone else for either of them. After they were old enough to realize they were in love, they swore they'd move heaven and earth to be together forever.

Colleen had broken that promise in the worst possible way, and it had nearly killed him.

Turning off the spray of water that had grown considerably cooler, Garret buried his face in a navy-blue towel. If only he could shut off the vivid memories as easily. He thought he'd succeeded in filing them out of reach this past year—until yesterday when he glanced up and saw Colleen standing there. She'd displayed all the poise and sophistication her mother had insisted she could have if Garret was out of the picture.

Garret wrestled with a million questions only Colleen could answer. One in particular haunted him. But he didn't know if he was strong enough to hear the blunt truth.

Deciding to get answers one way or another, he retrieved the clothes his mom had left outside the bathroom door and got dressed. Garret hoped his mother had taken the hint that he preferred to be left alone. He should've known better. Meddling was a family art. Indeed, Clare Logan bustled about, bringing order to his kitchen.

"Hey, boy." He bent slowly to keep the lingering dizziness at bay, and scrubbed Domino's head and patted his wiggling backside. "No run today," Garret said when the dog sat and stared longingly at the leash hanging next to the back door.

Crossing to the sink, Garret washed his hands before accepting the steaming mug Clare held out to him.

"I must say you look a lot more presentable than you did when I got here."

"I feel fine. You don't need to babysit me, Ma. I'm going to work as soon as I finish this coffee. It's good, by the way."

She snorted. "Don't you know by now that flattery won't get you anywhere with me? You'd say it was good if it was sludge, hoping I'll hush up and make myself scarce. And I will—eventually. I have chores to do before I join Kellee at our pottery booth," Clare said, referring to Brian's wife. Clare, Kellee and Galen's wife, Sheila, met throughout the year to mix, pour, fire and glaze unique pottery pieces they sold in local stores once a year during the arts and crafts fair. Garret remembered Colleen used to love to help, but her mother constantly complained that the chemicals in the clay would make her fingers too rough for playing her violin.

Clare broke into Garret's silent musing. "Your dad is driving to Knoxville today to pick up supplies the community club ordered for the Art Association's barbecue dance. Ride home with me. You can go along to see he doesn't overdo the heavy lifting."

Garret studied her through the steam rising from his mug. "This is Sean's morning to volunteer at the firehouse. I can't leave Brian to handle the pub by himself."

"Brian suggested I ask you. He phoned while you were in the shower."

"The way he bitches if he's ever left alone to tend bar and cook for the lunch crowd? What are you guys not telling me, Ma?"

Guilt pinched Clare's features as she avoided her son's dark brown eyes, so like her own. Inspecting her lightly polished nails, she finally caved in. "It's for your own good, Garret. On her way to work, Trish saw Colleen turning into the high-school parking lot. For whatever reason, it seems she's determined to poke around town. Maybe she'll find whatever she's after and leave at the end of the day."

Garret took a swallow of his coffee, which gave him time to process the new information. "She left White Oak Valley before she graduated. Do you think her visit has to do with that?" he muttered, finally setting his mug down. "Nah, any information she needed from the school she could get by phone."

"Garret, we were discussing you helping your dad."

Yeah, and he'd never hear the end of it if he turned her down. Not that he would. His dad had undergone a triple bypass the previous year, and the boys pitched in with heavy chores whenever possible. "Sure, I'll go with Dad." Besides, Garret figured it'd be smart to clear his mind before he talked to Colleen. "Give me a minute to let Domino run around the backyard first. Oh, and top off my coffee, will you? Then we can take off."

"Really? Fantastic." Clare sprang from her chair to get the coffee. "Do you feel like a breakfast roll yet? I used almond flavoring in the glaze just for you."

He opened his mouth to refuse, then decided to save his arguments for the battle that was sure to come when his family learned about his plans to confront Colleen—even if he had to follow her to Boston. One way or another, he'd made up his mind that they were going to meet again. Today, he wasn't up to a skirmish with her or his family, especially considering the way his head split when he whistled Domino back into the house.

But Garret knew he'd have it out with any or all of

the Logans if they interfered with his seeing Colleen. He'd wasted one night trying to numb the shock of learning she was very much alive. Now it was time, as his mother had said earlier, to act like a man. A Logan. Surely she hadn't forgotten what set Logan men apart from others. They believed in love at first sight and were loyal to that one woman forever.

There wasn't much point in inviting another lecture by reminding his mom of that fact, Garret thought as they drove into town. When they arrived, he glanced over at the house where Colleen Drake had once lived.

So many memories had been woven between them over the years, until his life had been shattered by the news of her death. Only, she hadn't died, and now she was back. Garret kept circling back to why.

Jo RECOGNIZED the White Oak Valley High School building from the yearbooks she'd found. Hope had faded that she and Colleen *weren't* one and the same person. And still it bothered her that driving up to the school evoked no memories beyond the photographs. While she had begun to accept that it was her picture in the yearbooks, and those were her talent awards, she wasn't able to fathom that she'd hurt Garret Logan. She'd never been close enough to anyone to hurt them.

Kendra Rowan had volunteered to accompany Jo to the high school. It was only after she walked through the doors and didn't know where to start asking questions, that Jo wished she had accepted the offer.

City schools had security guards at the entrances. Here, a person could wander at will. Jo stopped to study trophies in a case that ran the length of the main hall. There were awards for soccer, wrestling, basketball and 4-H ribbons. She looked for Colleen Drake's name but didn't find it. The name Logan figured prominently on a number of plaques and trophies. Jo concluded it was a big family.

In the office she was greeted by a woman working at a computer. "I came across some old yearbooks from this school when I was cleaning out a closet after my mother died. I just wondered if there are any teachers who would've taught here eight or nine years ago still on staff. I'd be willing to make an appointment to see someone after school or during a break. I'd really like to talk to them."

"Eight or nine years ago? The board offered a really great retirement package four years ago. Most people who were eligible took the offer."

"That's disappointing, but I'm not surprised. Thank you anyway." Jo had nearly reached the door, when the woman called her back. "Wait. Mr. Rice, our music instructor, came out of retirement at our new principal's request. I don't know if he'd be of any help, but he has a prep period that runs for another fifteen minutes. You're welcome to see if he's in the music room."

Jo's heart beat faster at that news. "I'll go straight there. Where is the music room?"

"It was moved to the annex last year. Take a left out

the door and follow the walkway. It's the brick building in front of the ball field. That made it easier for students going to and from the field for marching-band practice."

Some of Jo's excitement drained as she left the office. From what she'd seen of high-school marching bands in Boston parades, none had violinists. And a small school like this might not have an orchestra. But, as this was her best lead, she followed the walkway to the music room.

A man with almost completely white hair and stooped shoulders sat behind a desk, changing reeds in a clarinet. Jo felt no connection to the room, or to him. She hesitated in the doorway, wondering if she should leave. But her shadow fell across his desk, causing him to glance up. His pale eyes, magnified by tortoiseshell glasses, widened, and the clarinet mouthpiece slipped from his fingers. "Colleen?" The teacher jumped up and adjusted his glasses. "Heavens to Betsy, we thought... Well, clearly the papers were wrong." He brushed his hands down his sweater vest, then removed his glasses. "What have you been doing since you left here, child?"

"Growing up, mostly. Recently I've been playing first-chair violin with the Boston Philharmonic Orchestra. I'm currently on hiatus from that and from my private tutors. They say I should soon be ready for the Boston Symphony Orchestra."

"I'm so very pleased. You were the most talented

student I've seen at White Oak Valley. I did my best to nurture your gift. Your mother, bless her heart, had such a time getting you to practice the classics. We...she, primarily, despaired of you ever attaining your full potential. In those days, as I'm sure you remember, you spent far too much time hanging around down at the footbridge with the youngest Logan boy. You two were forever skipping out on church choir practice, too." Mr. Rice set his glasses on a book of musical scores. Resting a hip on the desk, he sobered. "Sharon realized she had to move you away from your next-door neighbors, or risk you foolishly throwing away all your talent to marry young Garret. He's a nice enough boy, but we all knew he'd never be anything more than a bartender. Part-owner of the pub, it turns out. Oh, my dear, you're frowning. Not every parent has the gumption to make these kinds of hard decisions. Your mother sacrificed a lot because your father had a well-established business here."

"Mother recently passed away," Jo blurted out.

"I'm sorry to hear that. And Joseph? Is there any chance the reports of his death were wrong, too?"

"No," Jo murmured through suddenly dry lips. "Dad died. I was first reported dead at the scene, but I pulled through."

A headache, one of the crippling kind that sometimes erupted behind the scar Jo hid with a full set of bangs, struck in earnest. She still didn't remember experiencing anything Mr. Rice had mentioned. However, he'd given her an enlightening synopsis of her family. In particular, her mother, someone Jo knew could be controlling. Her mother was fanatical when it came to pushing Jo to work harder at furthering her career.

But would she have gone so far as to concoct a background full of lies?

It wasn't at all surprising Sharon hadn't mentioned Jo ever having a boyfriend. She would never have approved. There'd been a few times in the years since the accident when Jo made offhand remarks about hoping to meet a nice man one day and have a normal life, including a family. Sharon had raged against any such notion. She insisted Jo was destined for greater things than marriage. Sharon usually followed that statement up with a lecture about how *she* had given up her own singing career to get married and have Jo. And where were they now? On their own, without the man who had sworn to provide for them.

"I have a class in a few minutes," Mr. Rice said. "Are you in town for long? I'm so glad you made time to drop by."

The sounds of students laughing and scuffling on the walkway outside the music room brought Jo back to the present. "No, I'll probably stay just a few days. Thank you, Mr. Rice, for taking time to visit with me. I appreciate it immensely."

He waved away her thanks and escorted her to the door. "It's a pleasure, Colleen, to know your talent has found a home. Your mother may have pressured you, but she only wanted you to do well. In show business there's a name for her type. Stage mothers. I hope you're happy, regardless."

"Is there a reason I shouldn't be?" Jo asked. Perhaps her old music teacher could shed light on why her presence upset so many people in town.

The teacher held open the door and told the incoming students to take their places. He turned back to Jo to say, "Happiness means different things to different people. I played with a band in my youth, but I didn't like always being on the road. Settling down to teach made me a happier man than the fleeting glory or better money would have. Your mother believed fame and fortune were the be all and end all. That's only true if being center stage fills your heart with joy, Colleen."

She stepped out into the sunshine and still shivered. It was so awkward having people call her by a name that didn't feel like hers. Jo pretended she knew what the music teacher meant, and waved a cheery goodbye. Several of his comments stuck in her mind. The main one—that Colleen had preferred hanging out with this Garret Logan over knuckling down with her music— struck her as odd. All Jo knew was practice.

The school library had copies of all yearbooks since 1945, when the school opened. A quick visit provided more information about the Logan clan. Garret, the youngest Logan boy, was two years older than Jo. From his photo, she recognized him as the first bartender she'd met in the pub. The one who had sent the beer mug crashing to the floor. For someone she'd supposedly spent a lot of time with—and ditched violin practice for—he hadn't seemed all that pleased to see her come back from the dead.

On the other hand, Jo thought, any girl would have fallen for him. In his school pictures he was handsome as sin and had a roguish glint in his eyes. Yesterday she'd thought his eyes were dark and mysterious, like a forest pond.

Already fighting a migraine, she shut the yearbook with a snap, irritated by this bewildering attraction to a total stranger.

But he wasn't a stranger to Colleen Drake. In fact, Mr. Rice said they'd been next-door neighbors. Didn't it stand to reason that seeing the house she'd lived in as a girl might be the very thing to crack open a stubbornly locked history? Jo drove back to the bed-and-breakfast feeling that at least she was on the right track.

It was almost lunchtime when Jo arrived at Buttercup Cottage. Jim Rowan was putting the finishing touches on a big chef's salad when she dashed in. "Do you have enough for a third hungry person?"

He smiled. "Kendra said you'd be back. She had me warm three wheat rolls."

"How did your visit to the school go?" Kendra asked as she entered the kitchen from the porch. "Wait, let's take our food outside. I've set the wicker table for three. Oh, and we have news. I rented the downstairs green room to a couple from Georgia—the Eberharts. They're nice as can be. I thought you'd be excited to hear that they'll be performing at the Mountain Music Festival. She plays a banjo and he plays something called a resophonic dobro guitar. I think that's right."

The name filled Jo's head with imagined sounds. Deep, melodious tones very different from the pure ones of her violin. She heard herself say, "Tennessee mahogany makes the highest-quality instruments. I know because my dad was a master luthier."

Kendra and Jim shared a blank look. "I'm sorry," Kendra said, "we don't know what that is…what your father did."

The picture in Jo's mind vanished. She rubbed at creases etched between her eyebrows. "I…don't know…what were we talking about?"

"Guitars. Jo, are you all right? You're shaking and you've gone awfully pale. Come, let's go sit on the porch. Jim can bring our salad and rolls. I'll pour you some sweet tea. Southerners swear sweet tea is the best pick-me-up possible."

Jo didn't resist as Kendra led her outside. "It's probably low blood sugar. I should have eaten that second crêpe at breakfast."

"Mountain air is probably thinner than you're used to. Here, take this chair." A frosty pitcher of amber tea already sat on the table. Kendra poured out three glasses and passed one to Jo. "I'll be right back. I'm going to go look up that word, *luthier,* in my dictionary before I forget how to sound it out."

She came back as Jim served up salad and parked a hot roll on each plate. "A luthier is a maker of stringed instruments. It's one of those four-dollar words I bet only people in the profession use. Your color is better," Kendra said after she sat.

"You must think I'm an idiot," Jo said softly. She pulled apart her roll, then wiped her hands on her napkin. Lifting her thick bangs, she showed them the pale scar that ran from the center of her forehead to just above her left ear. "You read about my mother's death on the Internet, but I guess that article didn't give any old news. Seven years ago, my dad and I were involved in a car-train accident. Apparently early reports claimed we'd both died on impact, but really the paramedics managed to resuscitate me. I lived, but was in a coma for a while, and I underwent multiple surgeries for internal injuries. I get occasional headaches that hit without warning. And…" She hesitated. "As I said this morning, I still have trouble with my memory."

"Like post-traumatic stress disorder, you mean? Oh, you poor thing." Kendra grabbed Jo's hand.

Jim gave her more salad. "My sympathies. At least I knew from the get-go what disabilities I'd be dealing with."

"I'm not after sympathy. I know Kendra had questions," Jo said.

"I'm nosy," Kendra rushed to say. "I figured something was wrong, especially after you didn't know Jaclyn Richmond. No matter, she's so not worth remembering."

"Kendra." Jim frowned at his wife, who merely rolled her eyes. But she did turn her attention to her salad.

Jo cut her egg into the blue cheese crumbles. Dipping a forkful of salad to her side of dressing, she said, "I'm so glad I stopped back for lunch. I really appreciate the support."

Talk turned then to the ongoing arts and crafts fair in town. When Jo mentioned heading out again that afternoon, Kendra explained which streets were closed.

"I hope I have time to poke through the stalls while I'm here. I'm moving into an apartment of my own when I go back to Boston. My mother never put pictures on our walls, except of me," Jo said, blushing with embarrassment. "I want paintings with bold, beautiful colors."

"Jaclyn Richmond's paintings?" Kendra suggested with a grin. Both women broke up giggling.

"I wish you'd move here," Kendra said when their laughter wound down. "It would be so nice to have a friend like you."

A profound yearning swept over Jo. She honestly had no idea what it would be like to lead a halfway normal life. All she knew was practicing and performing. "I have to get going," she said, jumping up abruptly. She carried her half-empty plate to the kitchen, found a phone book and was amazed at the number of Logans listed. She weeded out those whose names she'd seen in the yearbooks at the school. That left a Donovan. Tucking the address in her purse, she waved goodbye to the Rowans on her way out.

Again she'd been hoping the house next door to the Logans' would jostle her stalled memory. But the boxy, two-story structure had been painted recently, so she wasn't surprised that it didn't ring any bells. She knocked, hoping the new owner would invite her in. No one was home.

She left the porch and followed the stepping stones between the only two homes on the dead-end street. She came to a gap in a well-trimmed, flowering hedge and suddenly fancied she saw a dark-haired boy chasing a knobby-kneed girl, who escaped through the branches. Briefly, Jo saw herself as a child swinging down from the lowest limb of the oak tree that shaded both yards.

She blinked twice, and the child was immediately older. Her red curls brushed the brow of a clean-cut boy sitting next to her on the top step of the big white house. The two were whispering, and she looked happy. Really, really happy.

Then—poof—the vision melted away. In its place stood the silent houses, the sturdy tree and an empty veranda.

Summoning her nerve, Jo hurried up to the door.

The veranda ran the full length of the Logan home. *Had someone scooted across the hall? A woman?*

Jo quickly knocked several times. If it was a person—a woman—faintly visible through the frosted oval glass, she had vanished. Three more knocks brought no response. Had the snippets of memory been the result of an overhopeful imagination?

More confused than ever, she returned to her car. Her next stop, and possibly her last attempt to find answers here, would be the footbridge across the river in the downtown park. Mr. Rice had mentioned that Jo—well, she as Colleen—hung out there with Garret Logan when she should have been practicing her violin. She'd already conceded that she was Colleen Drake. Now she'd just have to live with the knowledge that her mother had fabricated a history and that she may never fully know why.

The therapist Jo had seen briefly had said when memory loss lasted as long as hers, breakthroughs sometimes never occurred.

That was a disheartening prospect. But she couldn't afford to stay here much longer. She needed to support herself.

Darn it, though, she was certain the Logan family knew something. They had to—she'd been their neighbor and hung out with the youngest son. What did *hung out with* mean, exactly? They'd been kids. It was very evident she'd ticked him off by—what? Dying or not dying?

Jo left the quiet, residential street feeling more unsettled than she had since she started this confusing quest. And what evidence could she really expect to find at the footbridge after all these years?

CHAPTER FOUR

THE PARK WAS DIVIDED into a soccer and baseball field with night lighting, a grassy area with picnic tables and benches, and an area for dog walkers. Hiking paths led out from the perimeter.

Jo had a lot to think about, so she chose to walk the one marked Nature Trail. Wild rhododendrons were in bloom. White flowers covered low-growing plants, but Jo couldn't name them. There was no traffic on the path and it was less than a ten-minute walk to the river.

The footbridge didn't look familiar. It likely hadn't changed much over the years. It was weathered, and had been built of sturdy wood designed to withstand the test of time. The bridge crossed a swift-flowing river at its narrowest point. The rails were worn smooth in many spots where people had leaned there to enjoy the view of the rambling, misty hills.

It was on the other side of the river, in a secluded fern grotto, that Jo found more proof that she'd been here before. There were many names carved into the massive trunk of what was probably a century-old oak. It was obviously a popular place for local kids to leave their mark. Inside a deeply carved heart, she saw the name Colleen. Smaller hearts led to another that said, Garret. In two other spots Cs and Gs were ornately twined together in a manner Jo knew she'd seen before.

Stifling a cry, she scrabbled through her purse until her fingers closed over the gold necklace with the oak-leaf pendant. In Boston she'd dropped it in her purse to keep it safe, and had forgotten it until now. She turned the pendant over, careful not to drop the chain among the ferns. The *G* and *C* on the back matched those carved in the tree. For the longest time she stared first at one, then the other, straining to remember. Eventually she knelt at the base of the oak, holding her aching head. *Why wouldn't anything come back?*

The joined hearts on the tree and the engraving on the pendant were significant. She and Garret Logan once meant something to each other. That was why her mother had taken her away from here.

Sharon had thrown a fit the day Jo announced she'd found a part-time job at a coffeehouse. She insisted Jo would be distracted by the men she'd meet and would lose focus on her music. Well, she hadn't met anyone, though she did look with envy at the couples who came in.

She knelt by the tree, recapping what she did know, trying unsuccessfully to call up buried memories, until the sun sank behind the hills, throwing the grotto in deep shadow.

When she finally rose, Jo fastened the chain around

her neck so as to not lose it. She paused to trace a finger over the hearts in the tree trunk. They hadn't been carved on the spur of the moment. Someone had invested a bit of time in them.

Like it or not, she decided as she started back across the footbridge, Garret Logan held keys to her past. While she might never regain her full memory, she deserved to know as much as possible. Good or bad.

When she reached her car, Jo noticed she had parked in front of an old stone church. Tall stained-glass windows and a set of elaborate wood doors intrigued her and drew her in.

Mr. Rice had mentioned that she used to sing in a church choir. What if this was the same church?

The sanctuary was huge. Hollowed-out niches held statues of Mary and Baby Jesus. The altar was set with burning candles and kneeling benches. Signs above two doors off to the side indicated the way to the offices and the confessional. So, it was a Catholic church. She and her mother had never attended services in Boston. Now Jo wondered if they had before. Her father's funeral had been held while she was still in the coma. He was buried in a city cemetery that, so far as Jo knew, had no particular church affiliation. If her family had been Catholic, surely she would have seen some sign before now. Then again, it seemed there had been many things she hadn't seen.

A kindly looking balding man with a priest's collar came into the church as Jo prepared to leave. The priest offered a bland smile, the type one would offer a stranger. When they drew near enough to pass in the aisle, he gasped and caught her arm. "Colleen? It's Father Hanratty. Mercy, I'd heard you were back from the dead, but couldn't quite believe it. Say you haven't forgotten me."

Jo felt faint, but it was obvious the priest knew her. "I'm sorry, Father. In Boston I was in an accident. It left me with gaps in my memory."

Father Hanratty patted her hand consolingly. "I'm the one who's sorry about that. It was such a shock to see you. We prayed for your mother when we heard you and your father had been killed. Your family wasn't Catholic, but you came to mass with Molly Logan. I can't count how many times I had to send Molly off to the back room of the pub to haul you back here for choir practice. Many in the parish lit candles for all of you out of courtesy. And now it seems our prayers were answered," he said, releasing her hand. "Is there something in particular Father Chapman or I can do for you, Colleen?"

Frowning, she nervously ran her hands along the shoulder strap of her purse. "Here's the thing, Father," she began. "Both of my parents are gone." She accepted more murmured condolences. "After Mother died, I found yearbooks from White Oak Valley High School. I've been building a career as a concert violinist in Boston. There, I'm known as Jo Carroll. I know Mother and Daddy's last name was Drake, but...I had no reason to doubt my real first name was Jo. I...don't suppose Colleen had a twin," she blurted, grasping at any possibility that might mean the past seven years hadn't been a lie.

"No. You were an only child. I can't venture a guess why anyone would choose to change a beautiful name like Colleen. Of course, I'm Irish," he said, winking.

"Mother and the symphony patron who more or less managed my career said it was safer to use a stage name. But I always thought that applied to Carroll, not necessarily to Jo."

"I don't know about violinists, but fans certainly mob other entertainers. Frankly, I'm not surprised to hear you've made a career in music. Although, when you lived here you tended more to play lively hillbilly tunes at the many wedding receptions in the back room of Donovan Logan's Pub. Three of the four Logan boys run the pub now. They still showcase bluegrass bands on weekends. None of the fiddlers I've heard can match your talent," he said. "Not that I spend much time at the pub," he added sheepishly.

Jo moved toward the door, then turned back. "Mr. Rice, the music teacher at the high school, said I spent a lot of time with Garret Logan?" Her statement was more a question since Father Hanratty had only mentioned a friendship with Molly Logan.

"My, yes. That's putting it mildly," the old priest said with a throaty chuckle. "You and Garret were quite a pair. Everyone assumed you'd get married after your graduation."

"Married?" Jo nearly choked on the word. Her mind couldn't reconcile that idea with the angry bartender who'd seemed to hate her so.

"You act surprised. Well, I suppose a music career demanded a shift in your priorities. Maybe it was providential that Garret was the one to accompany his mother to Ireland that summer. It was Clare Logan's first visit to her parents' homeland since she'd married Donovan. She did so want him to go along. But he's a stubborn Irishman who flatly refuses to fly. Still, he didn't want Clare traveling alone. Ah, well, but that all took place years ago. I've forgotten exactly how long," Father Hanratty said. "They may have been off and gone before you got that audition up north. You'd know the date far better than I. Time does fly, and my memory isn't what it used to be, either."

Jo nodded respectfully, but her head had begun to ache again. All of this was too much to process. Her brain had stalled when Father Hanratty said it was common knowledge that she'd contemplated marriage. The more people revealed about her past in this town, the more confused she became.

She wasn't yet willing to admit that her whole life prior to her accident was missing. "I visited our old house this morning," she said, thinking that was safer ground. "No one was home there or at the Logans' next door."

"A veterinarian, Pete Simmons, and his wife bought your old house. The doctor converted your father's workshop into his clinic."

"Workshop? Oh, where Dad made violins?"

"Everyone called them fiddles, but, yes, he made beautiful instruments. The whole town misses the notoriety of the famous country musicians Joseph had begun to attract. Really, musicians from all over the country used to visit here to buy Joseph Drake's custom guitars and fiddles."

There was that word fiddle *again.* Jo's mother would turn over in her grave if she could hear someone call a Joseph Drake violin a fiddle. "I'd love to see inside the house. Maybe I'll stop by there again tomorrow."

"They might not be in for a while. A few days a week Doc Simmons operates a mobile veterinary service to families in the hill communities. If no one was home, this is probably one of his road days. And if they don't have animals in their hospital, I believe his wife travels with him. Keep trying if you don't catch anyone home."

"Uh, I don't know how much longer I'll be in town. I may try to come back again for the Mountain Music Festival."

"Are you eligible for that competition? I thought it was a contest for amateurs."

"I don't plan to enter. It's…I came across a stack of awards in my mother's belongings. I…I…guess they're contests I won when we lived here."

"No doubt. Even when you were a little sprout your talent outshone musicians who'd been performing much longer."

Jo found it awkward to accept praise for performances she didn't remember. But he, too, had provided a better picture of things her mother hadn't told her. "Father, thank you for taking time to reminisce. I should be getting on. I want a word with Garret Logan before I head out of town," she said, shrugging offhandedly.

"How long have we been chatting?" The old man patted his jacket and found a pocket watch. "On my way back from visiting one of our shut-ins, I passed Garret and Donovan in the next block at the Masonic Lodge. They were unloading supplies for the barbecue and dance at the end of our arts and crafts fair. If you hurry, Colleen, you can probably catch him. Either at the lodge or at the pub. I imagine he'd be heading there next."

"Thank you again. I'll go there straight away." Fluttering a hand, Jo sprinted out and down the cement steps. On the street, she stopped to catch her breath. Did she want to confront Mr. Crabby Pants in the presence of his father?

How much worse could today's encounter be than their first one? After listening to Mr. Rice and Father Hanratty, she wondered about how her relationship with Garret had ended. Had she broken his heart? If she owed him an apology, she needed to get it over with.

She hurried down the street in the direction Father Hanratty had indicated and caught sight of Garret Logan's lithe body standing on the sidewalk a block ahead of her. He lifted a hand in salute to the driver of a dark-blue pickup pulling away from the curb. Maybe her luck in this town was finally changing for the better. Whatever problems existed between them long ago, surely they could discuss them now like reasonable adults.

"Hey," she called as he started to walk. "Wait up." As she broke into a jog, the oak-leaf pendant bounced up and hit her chin. Jo grabbed the leaf, holding it steady while she ran. She was gaining on him, and when she called out again, she could see him stiffen as he slowly turned to face her.

Not used to exercise, she couldn't catch her breath. She let go of the pendant to gesture that she wanted to talk to him.

She wasn't prepared for the pain and anger she saw contorting his handsome features. And even less prepared to have his tanned fingers close around the oak leaf. One yank broke the dainty chain.

Her hand flew to the back of her neck. "Ouch! Are you crazy?" she shouted.

Scowling, Garret wound the chain around the pendant and stuffed it in his pocket. "You've got some nerve wearing that. I resent the hell out of it."

"Obviously. Look, whatever I did to you when I lived here, I'm sorry."

"You think tossing off a measly apology cuts it? It doesn't come close," he snapped. "So, who was it who died in the wreck with your dad? You look just fine and dandy, Colleen. But what about the baby?"

She drew back and tripped over a crack in the sidewalk. "Wh-what baby?"

"Our baby. Yours and mine." He gestured impatiently at her. "I saw the test strip, so don't try to lie your way out of it. I know you were afraid of what your mother would say. But we both knew abortion wasn't an option. We agreed that when I got back from Ireland the next month we'd face our parents. Instead, you took off to Boston while I was gone. Did you cave and let your parents talk you into one?"

"I didn't, I'd never..." She just kept shaking her head, looking more and more bewildered. "Stop making up stories about me."

"Oh, so that's your new angle? I'm the liar? You know what, Colleen, I grieved for you. So did my family. So did half the town. I don't wanna hear whatever lame excuse you've cooked up. Just...just...leave me the hell alone, all right?"

Jo jerked as if he'd slapped her. Her hand flew to her stomach. Naked, her lower abdomen wasn't pretty. She had scars from two surgeries. Emergencies, doctors said. They'd removed her spleen after the accident, and there was a second surgery to stop internal bleeding while she was in the coma. That site got infected. They'd had to graft skin from her hip. But she would know, wouldn't she, if she'd ever been pregnant? Doctors, nurses, someone would have told her about a loss of that magnitude.

"Why?" she cried, her vision blurring. "Why are

you doing this? I don't understand. Did you spread these lies in town? Is that why people look at me funny? You said we had a score to settle. What did I do to you to make you want to hurt me like this? Tell me. All I want is the truth." Tears streamed down her face.

"Stop! You know that's the truth," he insisted.

"No. My life began when I woke up in a Boston hospital. For your information, I *was* in the accident that killed my dad, and I nearly died, too. Now both of my parents are gone. I found a box of yearbooks in the closet and I came here to try to fill in blanks. Because there's not a soul left that I can ask about any of this."

Garret felt his insides twist. "Don't do this to either of us, Colleen. I swear you took a pregnancy test and it was positive." He pleaded with her with his eyes.

"I don't believe you. I don't even remember you. At least I now understand my mother's reasons for not telling me about White Oak Valley. She obviously knew the kind of person you are." Jo clapped a hand over her mouth to keep from laying more blame on her mother. She didn't want to give Garret Logan that much power over her. She couldn't believe they'd ever been friends, let alone more.

Whirling around, she ran blindly back toward her car. Tears blurred her vision.

A car, a silver Cadillac with smoke-gray windows, swung onto the curb beside Jo, causing her to dive for the wall of a brick building. For a terrible moment she imagined screeching train wheels and heard the long, wailing blast of a horn. Sparks flew, followed by the terrible rending of metal. Dropping into a crouch, she shut her eyes, covered her head and waited for the train to hit.

"Jo Carroll! I've been looking all over this hillbilly town for you." Jerrold Cleary sprang from the car he'd left running. He smoothed a hand through his silver hair. "Stand up. What's wrong with you? Why are you cowering on the sidewalk like some crazy person?" Jerrold hauled her up and handed her the purse she'd dropped. "Why didn't you tell me you were coming here? I never would've known where you'd gone if your doorman hadn't remembered seeing you go into a travel agency in the next block."

"Jerrold!" Jo dug a packet of tissues out of her purse and blew her nose. She still felt off-kilter, but her racing heart had begun to slow.

"You look like hell." He parked his hands on his hips.

"That's just what I need right now, Jerrold. More encouraging words. Go back to Boston."

"As long as you come to your senses and return with me. I knew you were having a rough time getting over Sharon's death. But what in the world possessed you to call Conductor Cunningham and leave him high and dry for two performances? You shouldn't have requested a leave until I was ready to announce the news about your summer tour. You forced me to make a statement prematurely. Otherwise it would have been professional suicide to cancel private lessons with Johan Kaskaksian like you did. You'll be lucky if I can get him to take you back after the tour. Where is Sharon's car? Your bags? Never mind. Leave everything and come along with me. You'll need every second you can get to practice if we're going to have you ready for Europe in a month."

"I'm not going to Europe. I told you that in Boston."

"You don't mean it," he said, seizing her by her upper arms and shaking her.

She tried to twist loose, but to no avail. "I'm not going, Jerrold. Stop, you're hurting me."

"Listen to me, you thankless little witch," he shouted. "You may think you're a prima donna, but you're not one yet. Do you have talent to be the best? Yes. But you need someone who knows how to showcase you. That's me. I'm your Svengali. And in case you think you can walk away from me, I'll remind you I advanced your mother money to pay the bills that piled up after Joseph's death. I paid for your apartment, your food, your lessons. Who do you think arranged for your first auditions, and then secured your lead position with the orchestra? You owe me everything. Now, get in the car."

Jo went limp even as he shook her again. "Did my mother sign anything?"

"We had a verbal agreement. But don't think you can weasel out of it."

"In other words, you have nothing in writing that applies to me. Let go. I'm not going back. I've decided to leave Boston altogether. I'll take a job doing something other than playing music. I don't want to sit in a boring orchestra for the rest of my life."

"Sharon's death left you broke, and you have no family or friends. You have no one, Jo Carroll, but me. I think in the end you'll do what I say."

GARRET HAD BARELY had the patience to listen to Colleen's excuses. And what was that crap about having amnesia?

He wasn't familiar with the disorder, but it seemed a stretch to think someone could suffer memory loss for seven damn years. Colleen was just being...what *was* she being?

She'd left him a note all those years ago saying she was going to Boston to audition at some snooty music conservatory. That wasn't surprising. Her mother had harped on nothing else. The only music Sharon Drake had allowed in her house was classical. She spouted off to anyone who'd listen how playing mountain music would corrupt her daughter's gift. Sharon let it be known far and wide that Colleen was too talented to waste her time on bluegrass, and too good to throw her life away marrying a mountain man. Especially one who planned to serve beer for the rest of his life.

Garret would have gone on to the tavern and left Colleen to her crocodile tears had a speeding Cadillac not jumped the curb and made him turn around to check on her.

The minute Colleen's greeting made it apparent that she knew the driver, Garret started off again.

When he heard the couple begin shouting at each other, Garret's steps dragged. *Dammit, this has nothing to do with me.*

He walked on several paces. Logan's was only a few yards away, and still Garret hesitated. He strained to hear what the two were saying. Yelling, actually.

The back door to the pub opened and his brother Sean came out to toss a trash bag in the Dumpster. Sean waved when he saw Garret, and came over to join him on the sidewalk. "What gives with those two? Who's the bigshot grabbing Colleen?"

Garret spun around to see what Sean was talking about. They both saw the stranger trying to force Colleen into the car.

The sight of the stranger manhandling Colleen sent Garret's hackles up. Colleen had always had the fair skin of a natural redhead. That joker's hands had to be bruising her upper arms. Plus she was no match for his strength, the way he was jerking her around.

Ignoring his brother, Garret loped down the street and inserted himself between the arguing pair. "You heard the lady," Garret snarled. "She doesn't want to go with you. Take a hike, buddy."

"Stay out of this, rube." The older man resisted Garret's intervention while scornfully appraising Garret's scruffy jeans and faded T-shirt.

"We may be simple country folk here in White Oak

Valley," Garret drawled, his eyes darkening danger-ously, "but we don't smack around our women. And we don't tolerate guys who do, no matter what kind of fancy car they drive. Got that?" Garret forced the stranger to let go of Colleen. And by steadily poking his forefinger in the man's chest, Garret pushed him back into the driver's seat of his still-running automo-bile.

The man slammed his door, sputtering protests. It wasn't lost on Garret that he engaged his door locks even as he ran his window down a couple of inches. "She'll never get another opportunity like the one I'm proposing. It's the chance of a lifetime. If you really want what's best for Jo, talk some sense into her."

Turning around to look at Colleen, Garret saw she'd crossed the street and was running toward a compact car parked in front of St. Bonaventure. "From what I heard of your conversation, Colleen doesn't seem to agree with you."

"Who's Colleen?" The prissy guy stopped brushing at the lapels of his rumpled jacket.

"Colleen Drake. The woman you were jerking around."

The other man barked a laugh. "Maybe that was her name when she was a nobody. Her mother and I spent years training and polishing her into Jo Carroll, ac-claimed virtuoso." He continued to glare at Garret. "Look at her Web site—if you have the Internet in these back hills. You'll find that connoisseurs of the philharmonic pay homage to her brilliance as a soloist. She can be twice as big in Europe. Really big, like… oh, what's the use of explaining to you. You wouldn't recognize talent if it bit you on the butt. Now where did she go? I have to find her, or she's as good as kissed her future goodbye forever."

"You hurt her."

"Ha! She was crying before I got out of the car. Who caused that? If you care about her, find her yourself, but send her back to Boston. She's just depressed. Losing her mother so suddenly has knocked her for a loop. She'll sort it out, and realize where she belongs. The downside is, it may be too late by then for her to take advantage of doors open to her right now. Am I making myself clear?"

Garret was glad to see Colleen make a U-turn and head back toward the Rowans' B and B. He could volunteer to help this guy, or he could stay out of it altogether. For a minute Garret wavered between the two choices. He and Colleen—or whatever the hell name she was using now—had been friends for ten years before she disappeared from his life.

He'd been ten when Joe Drake bought the house next door. Colleen was eight. The day the family moved in, Garret had chased her home through the hedge, taunting her with a bull snake he held by the tail. She'd hidden behind the trunk of a big oak on their property and pounced on him, making off with his snake. She'd garnered his admiration from that day forward.

Love had come later. A love he apparently hadn't been able to shake.

"Something you should know about White Oak Valley," he finally said to the man in the Cadillac. "We protect our own. And until she says different, Colleen is still a Smoky Mountain girl."

Abruptly turning his attention to Sean, who had joined him next to the car, Garret stepped away from the window. "Sean, give Jason Colby or one of his deputies a heads-up. Tell him we've got a flatland foreigner in a silver Cadillac with Massachusetts license plates making a nuisance of himself on Main Street. I believe the fine for that," he said mildly, squinting at the stranger again, "is a thousand bucks or two nights in our rat-infested jailhouse."

The man peeled away, cursing Garret, who hooked his thumbs nonchalantly over a low-riding belt.

Sean closed his cell phone. "Mind telling me what that exercise was about? You know damn well Jase Colby hasn't been the chief of police in five years."

"Yeah. We know that, but Massachusetts doesn't. I just wanted to scare him into leaving town." Garret checked on the disappearing Cadillac, which was now following the route Colleen had taken.

Sean tugged on his brother's sleeve. "Tell you what. If you work the rest of my shift, I won't blab any of this to the family."

"Blab away. I'm going to find Colleen."

"That's a dumb-ass move and you know it."

"You didn't see her, Sean. It was like…she's been brainwashed or something. I just need to make sure she's okay."

"Garret, let the old dude handle her. You're over her, man. You're dating Jaclyn now. And you're almost back to your old self."

"Then one chat with Colleen won't change anything, will it? Listen, Dad dropped me off. I need to borrow your pickup."

"No. Oh, crap, all right!" Sean rolled his eyes and tossed Garret his keys.

CHAPTER FIVE

WHEN SHE PULLED into the driveway of the B and B, Jo was glad to see Kendra on the porch snapping green beans. Without turning off the engine, Jo stepped out of her car and called, "Kendra, I ran into someone from Boston in town. I'd rather he not find out where I'm staying. Is there someplace out of sight of the highway where I can park?"

Setting her bowl on the wicker stand next to her chair, Kendra ran down the steps. "Aha! I knew you were running from a man. Oh, but I can gloat later. See that dirt road? Follow it to the back of the house. Your car should fit behind the garden shed. There's a brick walkway from there to the kitchen door. I'll go unlock it and clue Jim in. He's working in the office, answering phones. What name shall we be on the lookout for? I'd better check to see he hasn't already booked a room."

"You're so nice. I'd hate to have you lose a customer because of me. Maybe I should find somewhere else to stay."

"Nonsense. This is our home first. If there's someone you're afraid of, we don't want his kind around, either."

"His name is Jerrold Cleary. I'm not really afraid of him." Jo heard a vehicle on the highway and cast a nervous glance over her shoulder, belying what she'd just said. It turned out to be a tow truck. "Jerrold tried to pressure me into doing something I don't want to do. Kendra, I heard other things in town that upset me. God, this is such a nightmare." The quaver in Jo's voice betrayed her anxiety.

"Go hide your car. You can fill us in later. Or not," Kendra said. "You sound like you're on the verge of self-destructing. Why not take a nice nap?"

Jo needed to pull herself together. Too much had come down on her head all at once, she thought as she drove around to the back of the house. Having Jerrold pressure her had been nothing compared to the accusation Garret Logan had thrown at her. She didn't believe a word of it, and yet he'd sounded so confident. And how could she be sure he was wrong?

Jo hated feeling sorry for herself, but gloom hung over her like an eight-hundred-pound gorilla. She parked, shook off the tension as best she could and found the brick path. It was a beautiful evening. She took comfort in that if nothing else.

Kendra met Jo at the kitchen door and handed her a tall glass of iced sweet tea. "I'm happy to report that of the two new reservations Jim accepted today, Jerrold Cleary isn't one of them. Do you want to help me snap green beans? I always find the repetitive motion relaxing. You're invited to supper, by the way. I'm fixing pot roast. It's Jim's grandmother's recipe. All of our other guests are eating out. But if you're worried about running into that guy again, you won't want to risk eating in town."

"Kendra, you are such a dear." Jo finished her tea, then rolled up her sleeves. "I'm not the best cook, but I can snap beans."

Kendra set the partially full bowl on the counter. "I love to cook. So does Jim. Did I tell you he and I met in culinary school in San Francisco? He was in the military, but he signed up for a class during his thirty-day leave. It was love at first sight," Kendra said, absently popping beans into two-inch lengths. "We hung out after school, talking about…everything. We had such big plans. Life doesn't always go the way you think it will," she said, sounding matter-of-fact.

"You can say that again." Jo leaned her elbows on a counter, built low to accommodate Jim's wheelchair. "But you two have bounced back admirably. The B and B is at least close to what you wanted to do." Jo tried not to look glum as she rested her chin in her hands. "The more I find out about my life before the accident, the more skeptical I am that my career with the orchestra was my own goal."

"But you play so beautifully, Jo."

"Which makes my feelings all the more confusing."

Most of the private rooms at the B and B were wired

with an intercom, and just then the one in the kitchen crackled to life. Jim's voice emerged through the static. "Kendra, Garret Logan is at the counter asking for Colleen Drake. I told him we have no guest registered by that name, but he says she may be using an alias."

Kendra glanced at Jo, who shook her head.

Kendra lifted her finger off the intercom button, silencing the static. "You have two men after you? How juicy is that? This I've gotta hear."

Jim wasn't giving up. "Kendra, are you in the kitchen? Logan says he's worried about Ms. Drake. Her car isn't in our lot, and he claims he has reason to fear she may have been kidnapped. Ah...he's not going away until he verifies whether she checked out or not. What shall I tell him?" Jim muttered in a more muffled voice.

Jo continued to gnaw on her bottom lip.

"Folks in town speak highly of the Logans," Kendra murmured. "But if you don't want to talk to him, I can send him on his way."

"We haven't exactly been getting along," Jo said, running her fingers along her scar. "Although, I came here to find out about my past and Garret seems to be part of that. Kendra, I wasn't totally up-front with you about...the accident I was in seven years ago. It robbed me of *all* memory prior to the day I woke up from a coma. My life before that doesn't exist, and it's scary."

Kendra's eyes bugged. "I know you said you had holes, but...wow, to remember nothing would be horrible. You must feel...defenseless."

"Exactly." Jo scrubbed her hands up and down her thighs. "When I visited the high school, I met my old music teacher. He said my family lived next door to the Logans. The first day I went to the pub, they were shocked. It seems the whole town thought I died in that wreck. And today Garret Logan told me some things about my past that if true are devastating. I can't refute anything he says. All the same, hiding back here with you won't help me regain my memory."

"If you're afraid of Garret—"

"No, it's not that," Jo interrupted her host. "He...said something that really upset me. Then he turned around and intervened when Jerrold Cleary tried to shove me in his car. I'll go out, so he can see I haven't been kidnapped," she said, making up her mind. She reached the door just as Jim bumped it open with his wheelchair.

Jim frowned. "Isn't the intercom working? Why didn't you guys answer me? Garret's driving me nuts pacing back and forth. He's ready to call the cops."

"I'll talk to him," Jo said briskly.

Kendra halted her long enough to give her a bracing hug. "There are no guests in the living room. Take him in there and I'll bring you some more sweet tea."

"I worry Jerrold may stop here if he's still looking for me. Is it okay if Garret and I walk in the apple orchard? I'll forgo the tea until I get back."

"Absolutely. How long shall I give you before I send the dog with the brandy?" Kendra said, in an obvious attempt to ease Jo's growing tension.

"Save the brandy, too. I may not feel like sharing it with him." Jo smiled at her new friends as she left to face Garret.

Garret turned at the sound of her light step. "So, you are here. I was afraid that guy had followed you and forced you to go with him after all. When I didn't see your car…I got really worried. I knew you'd had enough of a head start to beat me here."

"I should thank you for coming to my rescue. Jerrold was sort of my manager back in Boston, and he's not happy with me being here." Jo crossed her arms and rubbed at the finger marks that were beginning to show on her skin.

His eyes troubled, Garret moved nearer and bent to inspect her bruises. "Your skin was always sensitive. You sunburned and bruised more easily than any of our friends."

"And freckled," Jo added. "It's the curse of having red hair."

Garret reached a hand toward her hair, then let it drop without touching her. "You've done something to tame the curls. If I remember, you cursed those on a daily basis, too."

"Your memory is better than mine," she said abruptly.

"Let's go sit on the porch," he suggested just as she gestured toward arcade doors that led outside through the sunroom.

"I thought a walk in the apple orchard, in case

Jerrold makes the rounds of lodgings in the area and ends up stopping here. I'm not going back to Boston. At least, not right now."

Nodding, Garret indicated she should lead the way. They walked in silence out into rows of trees where fruit had already begun to form. Garret kept darting her sidelong glances as if waiting for her to speak first.

She studied the trees and the evening sky peeking through the leafy branches, taking care to keep him more than an arm's length away.

He finally picked a small, unformed apple and turned it around and around in his large hands. "Colleen, in town you claimed not to know me. I don't understand. I thought amnesia was temporary. How can our ten-year relationship have left you with no impressions at all?"

She fluttered her hands helplessly. "I have dissociative memory loss. For starters, I can't even relate to the name Colleen. I hear it and wonder if I'm living a bad dream."

"It's no dream. You moved to White Oak Valley when you were eight. You already played longhair music on a kid-size fiddle your dad had made for you. You don't remember that?"

"No. This is what I know. A little over a month ago, my mother had a brain aneurysm. She died before medical help arrived. She and I shared a two-bedroom apartment in Boston. As far as I knew, we always had. After I assessed my finances, I realized I had to downsize. While packing up her bedroom, I found some yearbooks from White Oak Valley High School in a cedar box in her closet. The box had Dad's name carved in the lid. Besides yearbooks, it contained award certificates from a Smoky Mountain Music Festival, made out to Colleen Drake. I figured she was a relative until I leafed through the yearbooks and found her name under pictures that looked like me." Bending, Jo plucked a blade of grass and began knotting it aimlessly. "At first I thought it was a cousin, or that I may have been a twin. Then logic kicked in and ruled that out. I came here for information. What I've discovered is a little frightening. As you might imagine, my life feels topsy-turvy."

Stepping out of the shadow of the trees, Jo flung away the knotted piece of deer grass. She lifted her bangs so that Garret could see the long, jagged scar. "This came from the car-train accident I was in seven years ago. Severe emotional trauma can cause dissociative memory loss. Most cases are of short duration. Some hang on, as mine has. Everything before the accident is a complete blank."

"That's so hard to grasp. Aren't there psychiatrists…?"

"Yes, and chemists and biologists. If biology, chemistry and psychiatry agree on anything, it's that memories are created. They aren't automatic."

"The day you came into the pub, you ordered sarsaparilla. It was always your favorite soda. We stocked it for you, in fact. How do you explain that?"

"I can't." She rubbed her brow. "Occasionally I have flashes that don't fit. That don't make sense. I think, wow, maybe it's a breakthrough. But, so far, no." She shrugged and briefly shut her eyes.

"I know you said your mom died recently, but holy cow, Colleen, why did you wait seven years to question her about your background?"

"That's where it gets tricky. I had no reason to. Mother answered every question I had. Now it appears nothing she told me was true. Not where I lived, went to school, nothing. She constructed a near idyllic past. Why wouldn't I believe her? I'm less gullible now, so maybe you can understand why I can't automatically believe your pregnancy story."

"Why would I lie?"

"Why would Mother?" she shot back, her hands curling into her thighs.

Garret threw the apple he was holding as far as he could to release his pent-up emotions. It landed with a thud several rows over and startled a flock of birds that had settled in the trees. Once the flapping stopped, Garret searched Jo's face. "Believe this. Your parents, mostly your mother, had high hopes that you'd pursue a classical music career. I guess she got her wish."

"That's no great revelation. I figured that out on my own. From the minute it became plain I hadn't lost my ability to play the violin, my life was a tornado of private lessons, practicing and performances. Even if she used my memory loss to manipulate me into following the career path she'd always dreamed of, I can't believe the doctors would agree to perform an abortion without my consent." Jo laced her hands across her stomach. "I'm sorry, I just can't connect the dots. I've never had a boyfriend that I know of. If I was pregnant that means that I…that we…" She couldn't finish her sentence.

"I know what it means. This is as hard for me to talk about as it is for you. We kept the news secret from everyone. We should've waited to…but we didn't. We should've been more careful, but we got caught up in the moment. So, we…just…didn't. And it was special. For both of us, Colleen." He reached up and snapped off another, bigger apple, and tossed it from hand to hand.

"I know this is awkward, Garret. Listen, I owe you an apology for the way I yelled at you earlier. It's so surreal. Of all things you'd think a person would remember, it's that." She gazed at him sorrowfully.

"Can you, uh, check it out?" he asked hesitantly. "I know what I know, Colleen. Er…do you want me to call you something else?"

"I like that name. I wonder where I was born," she said suddenly. "Not here, I guess, if you say I moved here when I was eight."

"You were born in L.A. Your mom was making her way as a jazz singer. Your dad made cool guitars, and one of her backup guitarists introduced them. Joe's business is why you moved here. His sales for a new type of guitar had exploded. He told my dad the hardwood supply was perfect in White Oak Valley, but your mother hated leaving the city. And she didn't like me from day one. She hated me even more when you and I started dating. Sharon made no secret of the fact that she wanted a classier career for you. She didn't want you to perform in pubs and she'd do everything in her power to see I didn't tie you down to life in a 'backwoods town' as she called it."

"I thought she resented giving up her singing career, but I don't remember her ever saying I was the reason she got married. I don't recall feeling unwanted, either. Compelled, though, to make up for her lost career. I worked so hard to perfect my craft, to please her. Mother chose the music I played. And what I played was way more important to her than to me."

"That's certainly cognitive thinking. So, amnesia doesn't affect that part of your brain?"

Jo stopped walking and glared at him. "You don't believe I suffer from memory loss, do you?"

"I don't know what to believe. You look so normal. You're still just as beautiful," he said, reaching out to trace his forefinger down her cheek to the small cleft in her chin.

Jo jerked away, saying coolly, "I may have fallen for your flattery as a teenager, but losing my memory has taught me to be far more wary."

"That's too bad. Your zest for life, your utter lack of cynicism were what I always loved about you,

Colleen." Because he had more or less backed her up against a gnarled apple tree, Garret threaded one hand through her new, sleeker curls.

His simple declaration rattled Jo. She scratched her elbow on the tree bark in her hurry to get away, and ducked out from under his hands. "Even if we leave my disability out of this, people can change a lot in seven years."

"I didn't get over losing you easily," he insisted. "Ask anyone in my family. It took a hell of a long time."

"Ri…ight!" She thought about the encounter she'd had with the woman, Jaclyn, who'd claimed to be practically engaged to Garret. Rubbing at goose bumps on her arms, Jo set off for the house. "It'll be dark soon. Kendra said skunks have taken up residence in this old orchard. We'd better be getting back to civilization."

Garret caught up to her. "I heard you tell the guy in the Caddy that you weren't going to play with an orchestra anymore. What are your plans?"

She shrugged carelessly. "Next week I'll phone the hospital where I was a patient and ask if there's any mention of pregnancy in my records." She still couldn't quite believe it herself. "I'll let you know what I find out."

"Thank you," he said stiffly, as if he felt as awkward as she did. "I hope for your sake that you don't find out your mother took matters in her own hands. What I meant, though, was how long do you think you'll be in White Oak Valley?"

She glanced at him out of the corner of her eye. There was a tone in his voice that made her think he might be hoping she'd stick around a while. She sighed, putting it down to her imagination. Maybe the years hadn't been easy, as he claimed. Nevertheless, his life had gone on, while hers seemed stalled.

"The last therapist I saw before I left the hospital said the simplest trigger could bring my memory flooding back. Since most of what I've suppressed is here, I'd hoped I could wander around and that some old haunt might do the trick. It's really peaceful here," she said with a sigh. "But, I'll have to think about making a living before too long."

"I see other guests here have gathered in the living room," Garret said, gesturing to the large window of the B and B. "So I won't tromp through the house. I'll walk around to where I parked my pickup. Actually it's my brother Sean's pickup. I need to get it back to the pub before his shift ends so he can drive me home. I've got a dog to feed, unless Mom or Dad went by to feed him."

"You don't live with your parents? No, of course you don't. That's naive of me. Most people our age live alone or with a partner."

"I live alone," he said quickly. "It's just me and Domino. He's a stray hound that showed up on my doorstep one day a couple of years ago. No one came to claim him. He's good company."

"I've never had a pet." She actually glanced at him

for verification. "I guess I should say I haven't had a pet in seven years. I lived with Mother because it made sense economically. Then today I learned Jerrold paid our rent. I hate that. But it was their arrangement, not mine. I'm not obligated to repay him, am I?"

"He admitted to having only a verbal agreement with Sharon. So, no, you're not responsible, even though he tried to suggest you are. Don't let him intimidate you."

"I won't. Twice since Mother died, I've seen a side of Jerrold I'd never witnessed before. Not until I crossed him. I suppose it's reasonable for him to expect to recoup some of his investment. Maybe I should go back to Boston," she said more to herself than to Garret. "Outside of playing violin, all I've done is fill orders part-time at a coffeehouse. Who's going to hire me without skills?"

"You can play at the pub on weekends and for special events. We sponsor live music on Friday and Saturday nights."

Startled by the offer, she laughed. "Sorry, but I doubt your clientele would be overjoyed to hear Beethoven, Ravel, Rachmaninoff or Schumann."

"No, but they love down-home bluegrass. You play a mean zydeco. You used to entertain at wedding receptions. Well, whenever you managed to sneak out of the house with your violin. As a matter of fact, I bought you a fiddle after sneaking out got too difficult. I still have it at the house. It's not as high-grade as the ones your dad made, but, wow, you could make it wail, Colleen."

Her face had brightened as he talked, only to shut down when he called her Colleen. She wrapped her arms around her waist and shivered. "I'm not the girl you remember, Garret. I don't play fiddle at hoedowns. All I know is who I am right now. I'm Jo Carroll, semi-famous classical artist. Much as I'd like to, I can't be anybody else." She hurried up the stone steps that led into the sunroom.

"Wait. I'm sorry to keep bringing up the past. Sorry if it makes you uncomfortable. On the other hand, you're the one who said visiting old haunts might help with your memory. I know all your old haunts. I'll be your personal guide. I work most afternoons and evenings at the pub, but my mornings are free."

Jo's hopes rose until she thought it over. "That's very generous of you, but what will people say?"

"What people?"

"Your family and friends. The woman you're dating," she said blithely, hiding the unreasonable stab of jealousy she felt at the mere thought of Jaclyn Richmond.

"This doesn't concern anyone but us. Someday, you should be able to sit in a rocking chair recounting your childhood escapades to a dozen grandkids."

"A dozen?" Jo burst out. Other than the number, the picture did appeal to her. "You're crazy, do you know that?"

"So, is that a yes?"

Warmth grew in her stomach and slowly spread through her body as she gave a solemn nod.

He smiled, but sobered quickly at her expression. "It'll be okay. No false expectations, all right? Let's say we're doing this for old times' sake."

"Only if you promise me you won't feel you have to continue if this becomes burdensome in any way."

He raised his right hand without hesitation. "I promise. I'll pick you up tomorrow morning at nine."

"Where are we going first?"

"Hmm. I shouldn't tell you in advance. Won't it be better if we let each experience unfold naturally?"

"Probably. I just wondered how to dress."

"Jeans. T-shirt. As kids we didn't go anywhere very classy."

That tidbit made her smile quickly and briefly. "Garret. Don't make plans too far out. You might not want to be near me after I phone the hospital. I know I said I wouldn't ever consider having an abortion. The me I am today is sure. What if we find out Colleen did?"

"We'll cross that bridge when we get to it. Should I call you Jo, then? You seem uncomfortable with Colleen."

"It's up to you, but at the moment I feel I don't belong in Colleen Drake's skin."

Garret rubbed the bridge of his nose. Finally he bobbed his head. "Tomorrow."

Jo heard him whistling as he rounded the corner of the house. She didn't recognize the tune. Climbing the steps, she put on a jovial face to meet the other guests at the B and B. She could only hope she was doing the right thing spending time with Garret Logan. What if she fell in love with him all over again? He'd implied more than once that they'd meant a great deal to each other. He stopped short of saying they were in love, however. And seven years was a long time to be apart. She was probably building castles in the air.

GARRET ENTERED THE PUB in a far better mood than when he'd left with Sean's pickup. "Well, you look like the rat that got locked in a warehouse full of cheese," his brother said. "Tell me our Massachusetts stranger ran Colleen to ground, they settled their differences and are now happily motoring their way north as we speak."

Garret slapped Sean's keys back in his hand. "Where's Brian? He forgot to post our schedules for the next two weeks. Kellee did make one out, didn't she?"

"Maybe not. Kellee and Sheila are working in the pottery booth with Mom. I filled in for you all day, which meant unloading and stacking extra kegs Brian ordered to cover the arts and crafts tourists. But that's okay. I'll take the day off tomorrow."

"I can't work in the morning."

"Why not?"

"I'm taking Colleen to Gatlinburg. As a matter of fact, I'll be showing her around the area every morning."

"What? Now I know you're insane."

"Do you know anything about memory loss?"

"Amnesia? Is that why you've lost your mind?"

"Sean, get real. I'm trying to have an important discussion here. Colleen *was* in the car accident you found in the Boston newspaper online. But they got one fact wrong—she didn't die."

Sean pulled his brother to one end of the bar, away from the few customers. "Is that the half-baked excuse she's giving you for dropping out of sight for seven damn years? Garret, get a grip. Why believe anything she says?"

"I spent the last two hours with her, and I think she's telling the truth. She didn't know me, you or Brian when she arrived."

"That's impossible."

"Try this on for size. When Colleen came out of her coma suffering memory loss, Sharon began feeding her a pack of lies. Colleen wouldn't even be here if Sharon hadn't died suddenly, leaving Colleen to find something Joseph had apparently hidden in the closet. It sounds nuts, but he had a box of old high-school yearbooks and awards she won at the Smoky Mountain Music Fest. She didn't even know her real name. Sharon called her Jo Carroll."

"You're right. It's nuts. But Sharon Drake was a piece of work. I still don't know about this plan of yours. I only know how badly hurt you were when she left, Garret. You're old enough now to do what you want, make your own mistakes. I just wish you'd run this by Mom and Dad. They…we all went through hell watching you come back from brink."

"They can't change my mind, but I'll tell them. They'll find out sooner or later. Colleen—I'm calling her Jo for now—she needs to visit places she used to know when she lived here."

"Garret." Sean made a face and rubbed the side of his neck. "You aren't a doctor. Shouldn't she be in the care of a psychiatrist? What if she's spent the last seven years in a mental ward somewhere?"

"You're really reaching." Garret grabbed a sponge and began wiping down the bar. "Someone should warn Trish before you get that second ring on her finger that you watch too many of those forensic crime TV shows."

"Speaking of rings, doesn't Jackie expect one from you soon? Maybe at the art fair barbecue dance. It's coming up pretty fast."

"She what?" Garret tossed the sponge back into a pan of soapy water.

"Well, that's the general assumption. Especially among the women. They've been shoving you two together for a year, and I think they want to see results."

"I've done nothing to give anyone that impression," Garret said.

"Well, that's what Trish says. Hell, Garret, maybe you'd better talk to Jackie."

"Okay. Next time I see her. But I assure you, we've

never spoken of any wedding except yours and Trish's."

Sean waved goodbye to the last two men leaving the bar. Both had left payment beside their empty mugs. He scooped up the money and shoved it in the till. "Funny thing, Garret, I didn't see you running away from Jaclyn until today."

Garret turned away from the probing look in his brother's eyes, his own mouth set in a mutinous expression.

CHAPTER SIX

AFTER THE TWO MEN SWEPT the pub floors, washed glasses and set up for next day's business, Sean drove Garret home. Garret had seen his brother talking on his cell phone once or twice. To Trish, Garret assumed. He should've known better, he realized, when Sean pulled down the long drive, and Garret saw several cars already parked next to his house. His mom's tan Buick was most prominent, but it certainly wasn't the only one. Garret saw both his parents climb from the car at the same time that Galen and Brian emerged from their respective vehicles.

"You've been busy," Garret said, scowling at Sean. "What, Molly couldn't make it?"

"It's her night to keep an eye on the craft booth. And you had to know this was inevitable. Mom called while you were unloading the dishwasher. She'd already heard about the mix-up on Main Street between you, the old guy from Massachusetts and Colleen."

"Sounds like a great title for the next country he-done-her-wrong song," Garret muttered, shoving open the passenger door.

"Maybe change that to a she-done-him-wrong song, Garret. That's more accurate, if you ask me. You seem to have forgotten the hell she put you through."

Inside the empty house, Domino barked furiously. "I need to take my dog out," Garret said, weaving through his family to unlock the kitchen door. "You could all leave now and let me get to Domino's nightly run. It'd save everyone from wasting time."

Clare Logan was never one to be put off when she was on a mission. When Garret grabbed the dog and petted him to tamp down the animal's effusive greeting, she reached inside the door and took the leash from its peg. "Sean volunteered to exercise Domino tonight." She dangled the leash in front of her number-three son.

Sean sputtered, but that petered out under Clare's do-it-because-I-said-so evil eye. That look had never failed to bring her boys in line. Grabbing the leash, Sean hooked it to the dog's collar. "Come on," he urged the droopy-eyed hound, "It's as well we miss the real fireworks."

Clare ushered everyone else inside. "I'll put coffee on," she said, and set about doing it without fanfare.

"Don't bother, Mom. This won't take that long," Garret said crossly. He threw up his hands when it became apparent his mother was paying no attention. "Okay, fine. We'll sit around and drink coffee." He took a seat at the kitchen table. "I'll kick off this discussion by reminding you all that I'm an adult capable of making my own decisions. I'm not planning to cut work to squire Colleen around. So, what's the big deal?"

Brian and Galen sat at the other side of the table. Both deferred to their parents. Garret's dad propped a hip against the counter near where his wife stood measuring coffee. "Son," Donovan said in his Tennessee mountain drawl, "You've no call to get riled with the people who love you."

Returning the coffee can to the cupboard, Clare set mugs around the table for everyone, including the absent Sean. "Garret, four people stopped by the pottery booth this afternoon to tell Molly and me about a shouting match you got into on Main Street over that woman. I'd say that *is* a big deal for White Oak Valley."

"Once, you were ready to accept 'that woman' as your daughter-in-law. She has a name," Garret reminded gently. He looked at each member of his family in turn.

"She does," Clare agreed. "Though if I heard right, she's not calling herself Colleen Drake." His mother let the coffeemaker finish dripping, then she poured coffee all around. "And it's obvious she's avoiding us."

"I don't know how much of Colleen's private affairs she wants splashed all over town. But Sean will back up my version of the argument." Garret explained what had happened. Wrapping up, he relayed what Colleen said about her memory loss.

"Amnesia," Brian scoffed. "Pretty convenient, I'd say. What daytime soap opera do you suppose she pulled that idea from?"

Garret bristled.

Shushing both of her sons, Clare shot a worried look toward Garret. "If her story is true, it's less than reassuring. We all picked up the pieces the time she left you."

"She's scared inside, Ma."

"And you have a soft heart. You think you'll take her to all the spots you two spent time together as teens, as kids, and the cobwebs in her mind will miraculously dissolve."

"It could happen," Garret said.

"Idealistically." His mother set down her mug and laid a hand on his wrist. "Let's say her memory returns. What if she still chooses her new life over the one she left behind here?"

"She could sure do that." Galen offered his first opinion. He always took longest in the family to comment at any family summit. "Women are unpredictable under normal circumstances," he added, flashing his mother a teasing grin.

Clare, in turn, swatted his arm.

"Look, I know you all have my best interest at heart," Garret said. "I can't deny causing you grief for too long after I thought Colleen had died. It was a huge shock, but I was only twenty. I blamed myself because I wasn't here to stop her from going, or go with her if it came to that. I couldn't get over the fact I was off having fun in Ireland, and I let her down. I'm still kicking myself, because if I'd gone to Boston to pay

Sharon Drake my respects when I heard about the accident, I would've found out Colleen was alive. This past seven years maybe could've been avoided."

Donovan straightened away from the counter. "Recriminations after the fact never serve any purpose. We're aware you've come a long way from that broken-up kid. We've had our say, and you've had yours. I'm satisfied to leave it at that." He polished off his coffee and set his cup in the sink.

Clare sighed. "Except Garret never had a lick of sense when it came to Colleen."

Her husband crossed the room and put a hand on the doorknob. "What's changed, Clare, is that now all of our boys are men. If we didn't instill common sense in them before this, it's too late."

She bit her lip as Galen and Brian followed their father's lead. Both younger men clapped hands on Garret's back as they passed him on their way to the door.

Clare was last to stand. She rose only after Sean and Domino made a commotion returning from their outing. Sean eyed everyone as he casually unfastened Domino's leash and hung it on its peg by the door. "I see Garret withstood his verbal flogging. From the sour look Ma's wearing, I'm guessing he didn't fall into line like a good little Logan."

"Sean!" Donovan glared at his second-youngest son.

Clare poured her untouched coffee into the sink.

She started to dump the grounds, but Garret took the basket out of her hands. "Everything's going to be fine. Stop worrying about me, Ma." Leaning down, he gave her a peck on the cheek.

She touched the spot, smiled, and as was habit, delivered a halfhearted slap to his broad chest. "Save the blarney. I'm immune," she said with a sigh as she gazed up at her youngest son's crooked grin. "You are so much a chip off the old block. Just be careful, Garret. And don't forget who loves you. I'm like a mother bear when it comes to seeing anyone hurt my cubs. I guess I'm not as ready to make nice for old time's sake as you are."

"All I ask is that you not treat Colleen badly because you all think it would be best for me if she left town. Give her a fair chance to regain her memory."

"I'll reserve judgment," Clare muttered as she joined her husband.

His family went out and closed the door behind them without letting Garret respond to his mother's last remark. She made a point of having the last word in any family skirmish. And his dad was right. Everything had been said. In time, he trusted Colleen would win them over again.

"That could've been worse, Domino," he said as he filled the hound's water bowl. "Ma said I'd be sorry for giving you a home, too. Now she treats you like one of the family."

The ungainly, odd-colored hound lifted his dripping

muzzle from the dish, nudged Garret's pant leg and gave a deep woof.

Kneeling, Garret scrubbed the dog's floppy, silky ears. "How about us taking a second walk, buddy? I'm too keyed up to sleep. Colleen used to be my best friend. I want that back, Domino. I want the old Colleen back."

GARRET SLEPT FITFULLY and his day started off wrong with a visit from Jaclyn as he rushed out the door.

"I'm glad I caught you, Garret. Follow me to Mildred's. I'll buy you breakfast."

"Can I take a rain check? I have plans this morning, and I'm running late."

"Planning to waste a morning on Colleen Drake?"

"I am meeting Colleen. Jackie, you know how much she meant to me." He slowed his steps and stopped when they stood next to Jaclyn's car.

"Honestly, Garret, where's your pride? Colleen breezes back into town, snaps her fingers, and you go running after her."

"Don't do this, Jackie. You of all people should understand. After Jake took off, and Trish and Kellee brought you to my parents' place, you and I talked each other through some tough times."

"Then have a care for my feelings. Even your family thinks you're making a mistake."

"Jackie, Sean's under the impression that there's more between us than friendship."

"Isn't there? Aren't we dating?"

"I'm sorry, but we've gone to what, maybe four movies alone? All the other times we've been paired up at the house or pub for my family's gatherings."

"Yes, but—"

Garret glanced at his watch. "Can we finish this discussion another time? I'm late to pick up Colleen." He opened the door to his Vitara.

"What am I supposed to tell everyone?"

"The truth. That we're friends who've enjoyed spending time together."

"Excuse me, but this past Easter, at Brian's house, didn't you say I had a lot to offer a man?"

Garret looked troubled. "I meant it, Jackie. Call me dense, but I figured after all the times I said how I felt about Colleen, you knew I wasn't looking for anyone else."

"Well, I didn't." She turned and yanked open her own car door, got in and slammed it, cutting off Garret's attempted apology.

He felt like an idiot. The first few times Trish had brought Jackie around, he'd only just started trying to sweat out his loss by clearing the land to build his house. Last July Fourth was probably the first time he'd sat and talked to Jaclyn. She'd told him how her marriage to Jake Richmond had hit the skids. And Garret had understood how low she felt. They'd fallen into a habit of commiserating with each other. And from his perspective, that was all it had ever been. He hadn't been too smart in the way he'd gone along whenever his family threw him and Jackie together. In hindsight, he realized, since he hadn't been looking to get involved, he'd wrongly assumed that Jaclyn wasn't, either.

Feeling bad, he drove off after her, and flagged her down on the country road about a mile from his house. He got out of the Vitara and she rolled down her window.

"I don't like how we left things. I never meant to hurt you, Jackie."

"I fell for you, Garret. What woman wouldn't?"

"You've known me since grade school. Did I ever hide my feelings for Colleen?"

"But she was gone. Dead…everyone thought."

"Maybe part of me knew she wasn't. Jackie, I—"

"Don't," she interrupted, throwing up her hand to stop him from whatever he planned to say next. "This is your night to close at the pub. I'll come by around ten and you can buy me a beer. Will you at least give me this, Garret? Will you let people think I'm the one who decided to end our relationship?"

He agreed, stepped away from her car and didn't return to his vehicle until hers disappeared around the bend.

WHEN HE ARRIVED at Buttercup Cottage forty minutes past the time he'd told Colleen he'd pick her up, several guests sat in the dining room eating breakfast. She wasn't among them. Garret hovered in the doorway, unsure what to do.

Kendra breezed out of the kitchen carrying a platter of steaming flapjacks and individual bowls of fresh-churned butter.

"Garret, you did come. Colleen just went back upstairs. She ate early so she'd be ready. And then she helped us in the kitchen, but she finally decided you'd changed your mind."

"I wouldn't cancel without contacting her. Boy, she doesn't have a very high opinion of me."

Kendra set down her tray and walked with him into the foyer. "I'm glad we have this minute alone before I call her room. I don't know Jo, er, Colleen all that well. I really have no business messing in her life, but to me she's more than our first customer. I feel a kinship with her. Maybe because I watched Jim go through his recovery. She's got a long way to go yet."

Garret listened to Kendra Rowan's rapid-fire chatter, but he wasn't following her train of thought. When the woman finally took a breath, Garret slipped in a question. "Are you saying she has medical issues I need to watch out for?"

"Nothing like that. Shoot, let me ring her room. Forget I said anything. She wants a big breakthrough so badly."

"I want that, too," he said.

She nodded, leaned over the counter, pressed the intercom and told Jo she had a visitor waiting.

"Do you think I'm going about this the right way?

I thought we'd see Gatlinburg today. The park tomorrow. Deep Creek and Roaring Fork for later in the week if she's not tired out."

"I'm not qualified to doubt your plan. I've spent a lot of time with Jim at the VA rehab. I've seen a lot of patients and families disappointed by what they thought were sure cures. Healing doesn't always follow a logical path."

Garret tried to fit Kendra's advice with his own vague notion of showing Colleen around some of her old favorite sites in the area. He was still pondering the right or wrong of it when he glanced up at a sound and saw Colleen gliding down the stairs.

Everything else flew straight out of his mind. She looked young and carefree, so much like she had the day before he'd left for Ireland. Today, she hadn't tamed her red hair. Unlike the sleeker version of the other day, now a cloud of fire ringed her face. She'd never had to work to stay thin and nothing had changed there. Her white jeans and blue T-shirt showcased enough of the womanly curves she'd developed since then, however, to make Garret's pulse beat faster.

Colleen's expression remained somewhat wary until she spotted Kendra. "Ah, you saved me a detour to say goodbye." She draped a cotton sweater around her shoulders and tucked a billfold in her back pocket. Looking nervously at Garret, she said, "Earlier I wasn't certain we were still on for today. If it's a bad time, I can stay here and help Kendra make up guest rooms."

"I offered that option only if Garret didn't show

up," Kendra hurriedly put in. "He was just saying that he's planned a fun excursion to Gatlinburg today."

"Half a day, right?" Colleen turned to Garret for clarification.

"I work at the pub from noon through closing. So we'd better take off if we're going to have time to poke around town and ride the sky lift up to the mountain observation point. You used to love the sky lift."

"I'm sorry, I don't remember." Her anxious look returned. "This may not turn out that well for you, Garret. Maybe we should just forget all this."

"Hey, we're not starting out negatively, okay? It's a beautiful day. We'll pretend we're a couple of the early tourists who flock to the corridor every year. What's not to turn out well with that?" He dug out his keys and moved Colleen toward the door with a gentle hand at her waist.

"When I passed through it on the way here, Gatlinburg did look intriguing with all its eclectic shops."

"You'll have fun," Kendra assured her. "Off with you now. I'd better get back to the kitchen and serve up the second course before Jim divorces me and finds a more reliable cook in town."

Jo giggled. "Like Mildred? Oh, but with the way she chain-smokes, I wouldn't be at all surprised if she's single-handedly responsible for the mist hanging over this valley."

"The mountains are about a billion years old and so is Mildred," Kendra said.

"You ladies are terrible. I'll grant you she's a bit eccentric, but at a billion years wouldn't she be petrified?" Getting into the spirit of feeling lighter-hearted, Garret held the screen door open for Colleen. "Have you been back long enough to have a run-in with Millie?"

"My first day in town she said I owed you an apology. I think she wanted to run me out of town on a rail. But I had the same effect on your brother Brian."

"Ouch. Sorry about that." Garret opened the Vitara's door and helped her into the passenger seat. "Seeing you was a major shock to everyone," he said as he got in and started the engine. "I hope you don't hold that against us, Colleen."

"How can I? You didn't see my panic attack when I found the yearbooks and music awards. I pretty much freaked."

AFTER ATTACHING her seat belt, Jo gazed out at the landscape wistfully. "I can't help wondering how soon I might have regained my memory if Mother had told me the truth. Now, is there a risk of it never fully coming back?"

"Is there someone who treated you after the accident who can answer that? Didn't you say you'd seen a shrink?" he said, getting underway.

"For a remarkably short time, actually. I was supposed to follow up as an outpatient. We skipped that, because Mother and Jerrold both stressed how well I looked, how great I was playing. Plus, it turned out that the afternoon the psychologist had available was the same time the private tutor had open. Of course, that could've been a line, too." She sighed.

"Let that go for now. It's something to look into on Monday when you phone to ask about…the other matter we discussed. The baby," he said, his voice a soft rumble.

Jo shut her eyes. "If it's true I left here pregnant and that gets out, I can only imagine what the people around here will think of me."

"The news didn't get out before, and it doesn't need to now, either, Colleen."

"Perhaps not. But it's changed my opinion of myself."

"Can we put that on hold and just enjoy our outing this morning?"

"Okay. I'm really looking forward to it," she said, suddenly shy. "What do you have in store for us first?"

"Don't laugh. It's silly, but you used to be totally hooked on reruns of *The Dukes of Hazzard*. Cooter's Place has gotten even more popular since Jessica Simpson starred in that remake."

"I won't laugh. I saw the place, but I thought it was a joke. They're dukes of what hazard? Cooter's Place…sounds…uh, buggy," she said, laughing.

"The hazard, I guess, is because a couple of crazy ol' country boys drove a souped-up car and they always got into trouble, but successfully outsmarted the law.

Though really it's because they lived in Hazzard County. Their cousin Daisy Duke was a fine-looking country girl. Insert there, well stacked," he said with a grin. "All Tennessee boys wanted to be as gutsy as Bo Duke, and we lusted after Daisy. Of course, the local girls imagined themselves as her."

"Did I?"

Jo felt Garret's gaze on her. "Daisy was blond, but otherwise I'd say there's a definite resemblance."

Jo shifted in her seat and fixed her eyes forward out the Vitara's windshield.

"I'm not trying to make you uncomfortable," Garret said, reaching over to tug her chin around so she'd look at him again. "I can't tell you I never found you attractive. And I'd be lying if I claimed that I didn't now."

"You *are* making me uncomfortable. Partly because you know things about me I don't know. On the other hand, you could say anything. The person I am today finds it hard to think I'd find those characters of interest."

"Call them hometown heroes. The burg, as we in the valley call Gatlinburg, basked in the notoriety. One of the original stars opened Cooter's Place. People flock here in droves to see the Dukes' smoking-hot car named 'General Lee.' Shoot, if you worked in a coffeehouse, you must've heard people discussing what movie stars were hot. Jessica Simpson and her sister, Ashlee, are just two."

"Mother said TV was a pastime for those destined never to be anything but couch potatoes. Suffice to say we didn't own a set. Because of that, I blanked out most talk about current TV shows at the coffeehouse. My coworkers just thought I was weird."

"Hmm. I can't wait to hear your opinion of Cooter's Place, and of Gatlinburg in general. I've heard it called tacky by outsiders. Yet some families come back year after year. And couples line up to get married there. Rumor has it the only other place that boasts as many wedding chapels is Las Vegas. Because of stuff like that, it's next to impossible to find parking on the street. We'll park in a lot at the edge of town and catch a trolley in."

Fifteen minutes later Garret was helping Jo off the trolley and pointing out the day-glo orange car anchored in front of Cooter's Place.

Jo followed him inside the old building. She inspected many of the thousand photographs on the walls featuring the original cast members. "Do people buy this junk?" she whispered, holding up a pair of Uncle Jesse salt and pepper shakers. There were wild T-shirts, wind socks, coasters and every touristy trinket imaginable hawking the Hazzard characters. In one area, a TV ran a constant loop of episodes.

Jo stood and watched for almost twenty minutes, entranced.

"We should move along. We're blocking other people's view," Garret said.

Startled out of her reverie, she moved along toward the exit. They passed through a laughing group of sixty-something tourists who reminisced about where they'd lived and what they'd been doing during what one called "the Duke days."

Jo didn't look back once she made her way to the sidewalk. She and Garret wandered on down the street. They watched the taffy-pulling machine in the window of a local candy shop. "That is so cool. I wonder if it would work to knead bread or pizza dough."

"Do you still make bread?" Garret handed her a piece of the still-warm taffy he'd stepped inside the shop to buy.

"No. Did I ever? I don't know why I said that. Sometimes things pop out of my mouth that don't make sense."

"You used to spend hours watching my mother knead bread dough. She taught you how long to let it rise, and let you bake it. Maybe you're beginning to remember," he said eagerly.

Turning, Jo walked on to a candle shop that had tapers drying on a string. She watched artisans carve intricate designs in some of the larger candles.

A display of stoneware in the next block caught her eye. "This is beautiful," she said, turning a squat pitcher around on her palm to better see the design. "It looks like a bird and the sun trying to break through the mountain mist." Examining the bottom, she saw that the piece was signed K. Logan and dated the previous

month. "Is this someone in your family?" she asked
Garret, who had strayed to the next window to look at
an inlaid wood table.

"That would be Brian's wife. I'm not surprised the
pattern caught your eye, Colleen. I haven't been down
here in a long time, but I think that's one you drew in
art class. You loved to come up with designs, but your
mother worried about your hands so you never threw
clay. Look around at the number of artists represented
here. Yet you went straight to Kellee's piece. This could
be important. Go in the shop and see if anything else
jumps out at you."

"Stop it, Garret." She set the piece down with a trembling hand, crossed her arms and hurried down the
street.

"What's wrong?" he asked, clearly puzzled as he
caught up to her.

"You're pressuring me, trying to force me to
remember. It's not working. And I hate how disappointed you look every time I don't. You think I haven't
tried? I've lain awake more nights than I can count,
trying to reach through the fog or whatever is blocking
the memories."

"I'm sorry. I hoped the power of suggestion might
spark it, you know, the way we jump-start a car. Maybe
it's something that simple, Colleen."

"I told you I never went back to the hospital therapist, but that doesn't mean I accepted my fate. I never
let Mother know, but I bought a couple of books on

post-trauma memory loss with money I earned at the coffeehouse. One mentioned that occasionally hypnosis can work. As scary as it was to think about someone messing around in my mind, I found one nearby and made an appointment."

"What happened?"

"Nothing. Just…nothing. She frightened me so badly saying that all paths leading to my past life had been erased, that I ran out of there and cried on a park bench for an hour. Maybe a portion of my brain was too badly damaged in the accident that nothing is capable of ever being recovered."

"I don't believe that. Do you?" He slid an arm around her waist and pulled her against his side.

"Sometimes, yes. And it terrifies me."

"If there are paths," he said, gesturing with the bag of taffy, "they haven't been completely erased. You said you've had glimpses of your past—like at the pub before. Honestly, Colleen, I swear I never meant any harm just now. I'm anxious. We meant a lot to each other. I want you to remember."

"I'd like that, too, I really would. I just can't make it happen. You have to be patient. If you can't do that, I can't be part of your experiment anymore. It's too stressful. I want to stomp my feet, shake my fist and rail at whatever gremlin is holding my past hostage. But I've tried that, and it doesn't work. Your plan sounded like a good one. You just have to promise me there'll be no more asking if I've remembered something, every time I turn around."

"I'll do my best. Now, do you want to take a run up the sky lift? Or shall we save that for another day?"

"Is there time? I don't want to make you late to work, and it doesn't sound like we should rush it."

"There's time. I know exactly what we need to slow the pace. We'll pick up a couple of box lunches and eat them after we get up to the vista."

"Oh, yes. That's a wonderful idea."

"So, we can be friends again?"

She studied him through her lashes. "I like the sound of that, Garret, I truly do. I don't know if you heard Jerrold say that my mother's death left me completely without family or friends. I'm alone and I could really use someone on my side."

"I'm giving you my word, Colleen. You can count on me to always be here for you." He tucked the bag of taffy in his shirt pocket, twined his fingers with hers, and continued down the street.

Two words flashed momentarily in front of her eyes: *Forever Love*. She tried to hang on to them, but as fast as they appeared, they faded. She wondered if she ought to mention the blip to Garret. While she debated, he abruptly stopped in front of a busy deli.

"Do you want to come in with me and order, or shall I surprise you with what used to be your favorite sandwich?"

"Surprise me," she murmured, crossing her fingers, hoping that a little thing like a sandwich would bring back her past.

CHAPTER SEVEN

"I'LL BE IN THE SHOP next door," Jo told Garret.

"Okay. I may be a while. Looks like there's a line." He took his place behind a family of four who were trying to choose from the posted list.

The shop Jo went into offered an eclectic mix of mountain crafts. She was fascinated by the array of handmade brooms offered in every size, shape and description. And by the baskets. She liked how some were woven with two different colors of wood strips. Farther into the store she passed mobiles, whirligigs and replicas of small birdhouses attached to iron stakes. These were yard art, the sign above the items said. Along the opposite wall sat shelf after shelf of jelly, honey and pickled local products. As her slow circuit took her back to the entrance and an array of dulcimers, she felt compelled to try them out, and found one more to her liking than the rest. The simple instrument's melodious rippling sound, the result of very little movement of her fingertips, was both soothing and pleasing. Shoppers gathered around to listen, which started her thinking about finding a way to make a living. She realized her thoughts leaned toward possibilities that would allow her to stay in the valley. Maybe Jim and Kendra would pay her to entertain at afternoon tea. She could sit in a corner of the living room and play the dulcimer.

GARRET EMERGED from the deli carrying two boxes that had been banded together with brown tape to form a handle. "Why the long face?" he asked as Colleen walked toward him. He halted his jaunty steps in front of her.

"It's my life," she admitted, kicking at the leaves that had blown from trees lining the sidewalk. "Do the people who sell crafts in these stores make enough for food, clothing and a place to live? Did they start with seed money so they own the stores, or what?"

"I don't know. The arts and crafts fair only runs a few weeks. Most artists who buy booth space there every year are like my mom and sisters-in-law. Talented putterers," he said, sporting a huge grin. "I doubt any of them make enough to live on, but certainly enough to supplement their other income. Why the sudden interest in our economy?"

While he talked they boarded the trolley again, and he motioned for her to disembark midtown where another line formed for tickets on the sky lift.

"I'm panicking about the state of my own economy," Colleen said after Garret helped her down. "What if I acted irrationally by angering Jerrold? He can have me blackballed. He's a very powerful philharmonic patron. What if I can't do anything but play the violin? Granted, I worked a few hours a week making lattes and iced coffees, but that doesn't pay enough to cover the gas bills."

"You can do lots of things." Garret handed her the lunch boxes while he bought the lift tickets. She looked so forlorn he was struck by an urge to make everything better. She'd always had that effect on him. Yet she always was capable and successful no matter what she attempted. Colleen had rarely asked for his help. In fact the only time he could think of was when she'd missed her period for the second month. He thought about the baby they hadn't had. Girl, he wondered, or a boy? His brother Galen had one of each; Brian, two boys.

Returning to her with the tickets, Garret touched on the seven years they'd lost. He'd spent two of them completing the house he'd once intended to give Colleen as a wedding gift. It was time they'd never get back.

"Speaking of long faces, what's causing yours?" she asked. "Are we running late? Like I said, we don't have to do this today if you have to go to work. We can head back to White Oak Valley and stop to eat at a roadside table. We passed a few."

"I really resent the lies your mother fed you," he said. "She played God, and she had no right."

"Whoa, buying two lift tickets brought that on?"

"No. Come on, let's go get in line and talk about something else. People are giving me funny looks.

They're probably worried I'll go berserk halfway up the mountain. It has happened. Once, a guy decided he could fly into the canyon."

"Isn't that a comforting thought. Garret, I'm far from happy with what my mother did, but what good does it do to be mad after the fact?"

"None. None at all. And it makes me angrier to think she got away with ruining your life and mine." He lowered his voice as they moved up behind the last couple waiting for a chair lift. The couple was elderly, and were accompanied by their grandsons. Twins of about four or five. Rowdy kids, running amok, bumping into anyone in their way. The grandmother constantly tried to rein them in, calling mostly for Lenny to settle down, but also his less hyperactive brother, Lyle.

"Is your life ruined?" Colleen asked, once the disruptive kids moved on. "When I saw you behind the bar my first day in town, you struck me as happy enough. You said my mother's biggest objection to us being together was because you never wanted to be anything but a bartender."

"Tavern owner," he corrected.

"Sorry, tavern owner. Maybe you weren't the one who said that about Mother. It could've been Mr. Rice—before you and I managed to have a civil conversation."

"You have no idea the hell I went through thinking you were dead. Just because you can't remember what we shared…" His voice trailed away, indicating a reluctant acceptance.

"I wish I could, Garret, and you have no idea how much I envy your memories. It's not fair. I feel cheated. What am I to do about it, though? Tell me, how can I catch up?"

She sounded close to tears. So much so, Garret tried to put himself in her shoes. Neither of them knew what the other had experienced, and he couldn't come up with adequate words. Instead, he reached out to give her an awkward hug. The lunch boxes she held took up too much space for it to be a real embrace. As he was taller than she, Garret settled for leaning his forehead against hers.

JO WENT STILL beneath his touch. It felt right to stand so close to Garret. At the same time it made her nervous. While it wasn't a new experience for him, it was for her. She stepped back. "The line's moving, Garret. Look, the couple with the out-of-control twins is next up, and then it will be our turn."

"Right." He took the boxes and passed her the tickets.

They'd reached the platform where they could see the chairs returning from the observation area. People offloaded quickly and others got on. An attendant closed the bar holding them in, gave it a shake, and off they went.

They heard the two little boys squeal in delight as the chair swung out into nothingness.

Jo shut her eyes and missed the initial liftoff from solid ground to empty space. She felt Garret slip his arm around her shoulders. "You can breathe again," he murmured near her ear.

She opened one eye warily and exhaled raggedly. "Is this really safe?"

"You have changed, scaredy-cat. This used to be too tame for you."

She edged closer to him on the narrow seat. "Maybe my equilibrium is affected by my condition. How high up are we?"

"Not high. The observation area sits at eighteen hundred feet."

"It is beautiful," she said, relaxing against him long enough to study the scenery. "Is that a river down there?"

"It's the Little Pigeon River. You, Sean, Molly and I fished all the good holes."

"Molly? Oh, yes, Father Hanratty said we went to mass together."

"My sister is a year younger than you. Sean's just older than me, so the four of us hung out together until Sean discovered girls. He was the ladies' man in the Logan family. He's engaged now to Trish Collier."

"Why is that name familiar?" Jo appealed to Garret with growing excitement. Maybe recognizing the name was a breakthrough.

"You've run into her since you got back to town. Trish works at the resort lodge. Sean phoned her after you showed up at the pub. I shouldn't admit it, but a lot of people were trying to get you to leave town again. Trish told you she had no rooms to rent. You probably remember that."

"Ah. Now I do. Darn. I thought maybe all this reminiscing had given me a glimmer into my past."

"Keep chipping away and it will." He pointed to an area of tumbling white water below them. "See those two sets of rapids? During the spring runoff, there are places where inner-tubing is fun, but also a little dangerous. You had to sneak out of your house to join us. Your mother was sure you'd break an arm or hurt your hands."

"Fishing and inner-tubing are foreign concepts to me. I can't believe I really did any of that." She held out her hands and they both inspected the fine bones and oval, well-buffed nails. "I wouldn't even know how to hold a fishing pole."

Garret ruffled her hair. "Back then our poles were just willow sticks we cut at the river. I did lift real fishing line and hooks from my dad's tackle box. But we tied them to our poles."

"I'm afraid to ask what we used for bait. If you say I put a worm on a fishing hook, I'll know you're making this whole thing up."

"I swear, you not only baited your hook but Molly's as well. Worms and periwinkles. You were quite the tomboy," he said as their chair shuddered to a stop several feet away from the observation landing deck.

"What's wrong?" Jo grabbed his hand.

"Look up and smile," Garret said as he pressed his head against hers. "They're going to take our picture. It'll be available in the gift shop by the time we leave. I know, it's a crass, commercial venture. Old-timers say all of the burg has sold out."

Once the picture was taken of them hanging in space with the Smoky Mountains behind them, the chair moved the final few feet and they stepped off.

Jo took a moment to get her bearings. The area had been developed to accommodate tourists. In addition to the main attraction, which was the unobstructed view of the mountains, valley and Gatlinburg below, the area also boasted a gift shop, snack shack and picnic tables. Garret forged ahead, staking out a table that had just been vacated near the far end of the observation railing.

"You know the routine here pretty well. Do you come often?" she asked, and was surprised to feel a stab of jealousy at the thought of him making regular trips up here with his girlfriends. But he was a handsome man. And unattached. It stood to reason that he'd had girlfriends while she'd been living like a nun in Boston.

Jo couldn't have explained why, but she especially hated the thought of him cuddled up to have his photograph taken with Jaclyn Richmond, the classily dressed brunette who said they were weeks away from getting engaged.

Garret didn't glance up from where he sat, opening their boxed lunches. "When I stop to think about it," he said, directing her to take the seat with a better view of the overlook. "I probably haven't been up here in eight or nine years. It's something we did as kids. When we got older and started pairing up, every couple claimed private spots along the river to make out," he said lightly and easily.

"Did we?"

"Oh, yeah." He let it go at that.

"I can't recall going to any river. What was our spot like?"

"It was a hike to reach it. No path except the one we forged when we first went exploring. A two-step waterfall fed a pool we, uh, skinny-dipped in."

She mulled that over as she sat and unwrapped her sandwich from the waxed paper.

He watched her with a curious expression as she bit into it.

She chewed as she rearranged the bread to hold in the escaping contents. Suddenly she noticed he wasn't eating. "Do I have cream cheese or avocado on my face?" she asked, embarrassed enough to dig through the box to find a napkin.

"No. Remember, you let me choose what used to be your favorite sandwich. I was waiting to see what you'd say." Garret smiled and bit into his own roast beef.

She stared at her sandwich, then turned to Garret. "I always get cream cheese, avocado, bacon and tomato on wheat bread. That's significant, isn't it? I remember asking for that in the hospital. Mother fussed and ordered me something else, but the nurse brought it anyway. She said it was excellent that a specific preference had returned."

"So there are bits and pieces of your past that aren't blocked."

"I never thought about it before, but I guess there are, especially when it comes to food likes and dislikes."

"Do you still order Cobb salad with extra blue cheese dressing?"

"Yes! Garret, I can't believe you know that."

"Don't get too excited. How significant is that really? I mean, does it relate at all to the fact you can't remember people or places?"

"That's the most frustrating part. I'll ask the psychologist who treated me in the hospital when I phone Monday." Satisfied, she went back to eating her sandwich.

Garret polished off his own and ate his chocolate-chip cookie as silence settled around them. "I'm going to go get us drinks at the snack shack. What'll you have?"

"Water would be perfect. It's getting warm, which I suppose means we should head back. Didn't you say you start work at twelve? It's got to be close to that now."

"Yeah. I'd skip out, but Brian would have a fit. I promised I'd hold up my end of the business if they'd all lay off bugging me about spending time with you."

"Oh. Garret, is my being here causing you problems with your family?"

"I'll be right back with our water."

"Garret." Jo knew she sounded exasperated. She glared at his back, then began gathering their mess. She tried putting herself in his family's position. Of course they wouldn't be pleased to have her show up out of the blue. Her disappearance had clearly hurt him very much. How could they trust her not to hurt him again? She'd been enjoying the day so much, but had been totally naive.

Garret had assured her only the two of them knew about the baby, but pregnancy didn't happen by osmosis. And he'd just said they had a special, very private place by the river. The sheltered life she'd led since waking up in that hospital made it difficult to understand how things must've been back here, back then.

She got up and tossed all but her chocolate-chip cookie in the trash. That was another food preference that had probably not changed.

As she bit into the cookie, Jo watched the twins, Lenny and Lyle, who had ridden up in the chair in front of her and Garret. The boys chased each other around the observation deck. Their grandmother had her hands full trying to get them to slow down. Her husband stood at the rail, peering through one of several viewfinders trained on the town below.

Garret returned carrying two bottles of water, and Jo's attention was no longer on the twins.

"Good thing you saved a napkin," Garret said, planting a foot on the bench beside her. "You're chocolate from ear to ear." He took the napkin, dampened a corner and swiped the edges of her mouth.

She batted at his hand, but a commotion at the rail diverted Garret's attention.

One of the little boys had climbed onto the rail. He'd taken both hands off, challenging his grandmother, who stood with his brother, saying, "Lenny, get down from there this instant. It's not safe!"

Lenny lost his balance and began flailing his arms. A host of bystanders watched openmouthed as the boy toppled over the edge. A collective gasp of shock rose from the paralyzed crowd. The grandmother's scream brought her husband running. The less rambunctious twin started to sob.

Garret dropped his water bottle. It fell on its side, splashing icy water all over Jo. She was stunned, not from the wet or the cold, but from seeing Garret vault over the rail.

Around her people rushed forward, blocking her view. She couldn't have moved anyway. She heard Lenny's screech of terror. She distinguished Garret's boots striking rock as he slid down the slope. Except she was seeing a train engine barreling down a hot, glittering track toward her. The image had appeared before in nightmares, but never as starkly realistic. And this time she was in the driver's seat, and heard her father's voice yelling at her to get out. Jo leaped up and was bumped

from behind, knocking her water bottle out of her hand.
She felt her knees give way. She slumped to the ground,
trying desperately to hang on to the images swirling in
her head.

The entire episode was over in a matter of seconds.
Two attendants who had been sweeping the deck took
charge of the frantic grandmother. Another tended to
Jo and shook her out of her faint.

Blinking up into eyes she didn't recognize, she
fought to get loose from the stranger. Her ears stopped
ringing as the scene at the rail came slowly into focus,
landing her back in the here and now.

"My God," she exclaimed. "Garret! Is he all right?"
Pushing away from the woman trying to help her, Jo
fought her way to the rail. The sandwich and cookie
were doing somersaults in her stomach.

She was relieved to see that several men from the
crowd had formed a human chain stretching down the
rocky slope. One man clasped Garret's wrist. In his
other arm, Garret cradled the sobbing little boy. His
whole focus centered on the child as he inched his way
back up the steep hill to the safety of the platform.

Jo's knees knocked and her legs wobbled. Garret
could've been killed. Accidents happened before you
knew it. Like hers had.

The grandparents and the others in the group were
applauding Garret, praising him for his bravery.

Moving well back from the fray, she sank down on
a bench. Jo felt mad at him for risking his life. Slowly,

it began to register how Garret knelt on the rough planks comforting the boy, who still held him in a stranglehold.

Their child would've been a couple of years older than Lenny. It struck Jo that Garret would've made a wonderful father.

She jumped up, unable to continue watching the touching scene. Jo turned to the employee who was still keeping an eye on her. "I came up the lift with the man who rescued the child. He needs to get to work and I can't stay. I have to go down to where I can breathe better. Please tell him I…ah…will find my own way home."

"You should wait," the woman advised. "You're white as a sheet. I understand how scared you must've been when your man jumped over the rail, but he's all right. There are hiking trails all over these hills, so if he's a local, he probably wasn't in as much danger as it appeared."

Her last attempt at dispensing calming wisdom bounced off Jo's slumped shoulders. She wove through the crowd of people and hopped on an empty chair that would take her down.

DUSTY AND SWEATY from his rescue mission, Garret separated himself from the frightened, clinging boy as soon as he was able to hand him over to the man Garret learned was the twins' great-grandfather.

"We're visiting from Texas," the man said. "Our

grandson warned us the boys were a handful together. Peg and I raised five sons. We thought we could handle about anything kids could think up. I've been stubborn about admitting I'm not as young as I once was. I can't thank you enough. Can Peg and I take you to dinner? Steak in the best steakhouse in town?"

Embarrassed by the effusive thanks, Garret shook his head and began casting about for a way to escape. "No need for more than a thank-you. I've, ah, got to find my friend and head to work. I don't want to rush you, but the boys would probably get over the trauma more easily with a soft ice cream cone down in Gatlinburg."

He saw the table where he and Colleen had been sitting. It was empty except for their water bottles. Making his way there, Garret grabbed the still-damp napkin and tried to wipe off the blood drying along a deep scratch on his left arm. His heart had finally slowed from the adrenaline. It sped up again when a stout woman rushed over to say, "The pretty lady you were with…the one with curly red hair…she's gone down."

"Gone down?"

The woman nodded. "She fainted dead away. Dropped right here at the table like a rock. I splashed her face with some of your water. She came around, but still looked peaked."

Garret conducted his own frantic search of the crowd with his eyes. "Uh, all right. I acted on instinct. It probably seemed risky to her. Thanks. I'll catch up with her at the bottom." He smiled and edged toward the line for the chair lift.

"No, sir, she said to tell you she'd find her own way home. That was after she mentioned that you had to get to work."

Uttering a few choice swear words under his breath at the reminder, Garret checked his watch and found he'd only make it to the pub on time if he used his new status as hero to go to the front of the line.

He wouldn't trade on that, and still he expected to see Colleen waiting for him at the bottom. Disappointment washed over him when it became obvious she had left. The man who'd taken their picture on the lift flagged Garret down. Calling himself three kinds of fool for wanting this memento, Garret paid for the photograph the cashier slipped into a decorative folder. He fumed as he rode the trolley to his car. Why on earth would she take a cab to White Oak Valley, after making it clear that money was an issue?

Garret knew what he'd promised his family. He knew Brian would already be watching the clock and growling at being left alone to deal with the lunch crowd.

But he'd just found Colleen again, and he damn sure wasn't going to let her slip through his fingers.

Swinging into his SUV, he punched the speed dial on his cell to call the pub. "Brian, it's Garret. Sorry, but I'm running late. Before you chew my head off, listen to me. A kid about the age of your Brody fell over the rail at the top of the sky lift and I had to go after him."

At the other end, his brother's bluster fizzled. "That must have been showy. I bet Colleen was plenty impressed."

"Don't start. I'll be in after I stop at the house and get a pair of jeans without burrs. Those suckers are tearing up my legs." He hung up knowing full well his first stop would be the bed-and-breakfast.

He roared into the B and B parking lot, flew out of the Vitara, and burst through the front door. Jim and Kendra Rowan were working at the reception area and got big-eyed at his sudden appearance.

"Where is Colleen?" he shouted, slamming his grimy hands on the counter.

"She went up to her room," Kendra said. "Hey, we hear congratulations are in order. She said you saved a little boy's life."

Garret refused to be distracted. "Something scared the crap out of her and sent her off down the mountain. I have to talk to her."

Kendra bit her lower lip and shook her head.

"Please." His voice softened and cracked. "I lost her once. I can't fix the problem when I don't know what's wrong. I just need to see her. If she throws me out, I'll go. You have my word."

Jim Rowan skidded around the counter on his back wheels. "Don't cause a scene. We have other guests to consider. Jo is upstairs, first door on the left. If there's any shouting, Kendra will come up and boot your butt out of here. Understood?"

"I'm actually happy to hear she's got people in her corner. My family…are sort of down on her. Thanks. I won't abuse your hospitality." Garret bounded up the stairs in spite of the aches beginning to form from his exertion on the mountain.

He paused at the door and took a minute to curb his impatience. After a deep breath, he knocked lightly. When Colleen opened her door, the look on her face told him he was the last person she expected to see.

She tried to shut the door, but Garret wedged the toe of one scruffy, dusty boot over the threshold.

"You're already twenty minutes late for work," she said.

"Why did you take off? What did you expect me to do? Leave a frightened child clinging to the side of the mountain?"

She backed away from him to stand at the window. He followed, but didn't crowd her.

"Of course that's not what I want, Garret. You were so good at calming him after the fall," she said, almost accusingly.

"He wouldn't let me go. He'd been showing off. He screwed up and knew it. What's this really about, Colleen?"

"You should have children of your own, Garret." Her voice rose. "You *would* have a child if I hadn't done whatever it is I did. Up there on the mountain, after I realized you'd jumped over the rail and could be killed, I had a flashback. One where I saw the train hurtling toward me. It's happened before, but this time I was the driver. I heard Dad yelling. Then I blacked out. I'm not sure for how long. Garret, when I woke up in the hospital, everyone told me I was a passenger. Even Mother said Dad was driving me to my class at the conservatory."

She was crying openly now. Garret didn't know what to do. He didn't know what to say to ease her distress. He took her in his arms much the same way he had comforted Lenny, swaying with her until her tears were spent.

"I honestly don't know what this means," he murmured. "I think it's good news that a window opened for you today, however briefly. Like you said, I'm very late for work already. I'll only go if you promise me you'll stay in town. We can work together until you remember everything. Will you do that?"

She nodded, easing out of his arms. "I came here planning to pack and go. I won't leave, Garret. I want my life back. If staying has one chance in a million of giving me that, I won't run away."

"I could always count on you to be honest, Colleen."

She ran her tongue over her tear-salty lips and dredged up a smile. "Don't take this wrong then, Garret. But you could smell better. Especially if you're going straight to work."

He threw back his head and laughed. Just as quickly, he leaned forward and pressed a kiss on her upturned lips. Then he was gone—clattering down the stairs, humming off-key.

"That must've gone well," Kendra said, following him to the porch as he left.

"I feel like a man who's been given a new lease on life." He waved at Kendra and to Colleen who stood at the upstairs window. Then, he got in the Vitara and drove away.

CHAPTER EIGHT

JO FELT SILLY when she realized she was still standing at her window with her hand raised in farewell long after Garret disappeared from view. Her thoughts were jumbled and confused. Until their conversation that afternoon, she hadn't given any thought to the effect her apparent death would've had on the people who'd known her.

She'd believed she was the only one affected by her memory loss. Her mother had always made it sound as if their family was completely self-contained. Call her naive, but she hadn't questioned it.

There was so much she'd do differently if she could only turn back the clock. In seven years she'd never gone out alone with a man her age. Using her vulnerability and the debilitating migraines that struck without warning as an excuse, Sharon or Jerrold had accompanied her nearly everywhere, except the coffeehouse. And her mother had even objected to that.

If today's outing was a date, it was her first. So, too, his kiss. Garret didn't understand that everything they did today was new ground for her.

"Knock, knock," Kendra said at Jo's open door. "Garret left in good spirits. When you didn't come down, I thought I should see how you were doing. I know you were upset earlier."

"I acted rashly, Kendra. Garret's only trying to help me."

"I hear a 'but.' Is it all too much, too fast?"

"Maybe. He has our entire history to draw on. Apparently, he and I were, ah, intimate in the past. And I'm comfortable around him to a degree. Then…he kissed me. It definitely wasn't passionate. If anything, he acted blasé. But to me it was more than a simple kiss, because it was my first. Am I making any sense at all here, Kendra?" she asked, throwing up her hands.

"Yeah. Jo, I spent a fair amount of time in the rehab center with Jim. There were a lot of military personnel who'd suffered serious head traumas. Their families and friends wanted them to be the way they were before the injury. They had difficult times coming to terms with the new reality. It takes a lot of patience."

"Did you see any miraculous recoveries?"

"A few," Kendra said, offering a sympathetic smile.

"Well, that's a relief. Garret's putting himself out, investing so much of his spare time. I promised him I wouldn't give up. But until you popped in, I was having second thoughts. What if he's doing what any old pal would do, and I end up wanting more?"

"What's Mr. Wonderful got planned for you next?"

Jo laughed. "Now that you mention it, he didn't set up anything. See, there I go worrying for naught. I was reading more into a little kiss than there was. I feel better. What do you say we go change bedding and clean rooms? Remember I said I'd help you this afternoon."

"You're a guest, Jo. That's not why I came to see you."

"I know." Jo linked her arm through Kendra's. "I need to occupy my mind. I'm used to practicing up to nine hours a day. You've no idea how good it is to think about other stuff for a change."

"I won't turn you down again. With two of us and only four rooms, we'll be done in nothing flat. Then we can talk about having fun."

The women soon discovered they worked well together and enjoyed the camaraderie. "Yesterday, making up rooms took me more than twice as long. Now I have time to plan breakfast menus for next week, and do the marketing for what Jim will need for Sunday and Monday meals. I asked him to look at the budget to see if we can afford to put you on the payroll, Jo."

"Really? Oh, but I can't have you putting a strain on your budget."

"Minimum wage. Part-time. I can use another pair of hands. I'd love it if we could hire you to play music on weekends. I'm thinking a wind-down period of an hour or so after guests come back from dinner in town. Jim said to ask you if fifty dollars a night would be insulting."

"Kendra, are you twisting his arm? Because if you asked me, I'd play for free until I have to leave."

"I have two ulterior motives. First, I want you to stay in White Oak Valley, and maybe this will buy you a few extra weeks. The other reason is I'd like Jim to get back to playing piano. He used to be good at it, and it's excellent therapy. He might not be so self-conscious if he didn't have to play alone."

"In that case, you've got yourself a violinist. And I know just what I'll do with my first paycheck. I saw the most fabulous dulcimers in a shop in Gatlinburg. Obviously I can't be sure, but I have a feeling I used to play one."

"Then it's settled. You're on Buttercup Cottage payroll." Kendra stuck out her hand and the women shook on the deal. The cell phone Kendra had dropped in her apron pocket began playing a jazzy tune. "Hello," she said. "Oh, Garret. I expected it'd be Jim calling. No, she's not in her room, she's been helping me. Hang on, she's right here." Kendra passed the phone to Jo, whispering that she'd see her downstairs.

Jo nodded before focusing on Garret. "I was going to ask if you'd made it to work yet, but I hear all the background noise. So, what's up?"

"I raced home, showered and squeaked into the pub forty minutes late. Once Brian finished chewing me out for breaking my promise on the first day, it dawned on me that we never talked about what's next. Saturdays are when Brian, Sean and I do the heavy cleaning around here. We open at six for the dinner hour. Why don't you come catch our live performers? I'll hitch a ride to work, and you can take me home."

"Sorry, I have a job playing after-dinner music at the B and B."

"Since when?"

"Since about five minutes ago. I'm playing Sunday evening, too."

"Well, damn. Our family always has Sunday dinner at the folks' place. I figured that might be too much for you to handle, but how about if I pick you up for morning mass. Nine forty-five?"

"I know Father Hanratty said I went to mass with your sister, although I don't remember it. Sunday has always been just another practice day for me."

"Your parents weren't churchgoers. You started going to mass with Molly because you were curious. After you and I began dating, choir practice was a convenient excuse for us to be together one night a week. I probably shouldn't tell you this over the phone, but we planned to be married at St. Bonaventure. You always said we'd raise our kids Catholics, Colleen."

"A week ago that would've shocked me. Don't take this wrong, but it's difficult for me to picture myself as a bride. I have to know...did our discussions about marriage only come up after we learned I was pregnant?"

"No way. I proposed right after I graduated and went to work full-time at the pub. We just never said anything to your folks."

"Did we ever plan an actual wedding?" she asked hesitantly.

"Only in the most general terms. We definitely both wanted our reception to be at the pub, but we never had a specific date. You asked the Silvermans if they'd play for us. Everyone who gets married in White Oak Valley has a buffet and dance."

"Who are the Silvermans?"

"Ron, Laurie and Zeke are a family of local musicians. They call themselves purists when it comes to mountain music. When they aren't recording in Nashville or on tour, they live out beyond Pigeon Forge. You met when Ron judged at the Mountain Music Festival. It was you who convinced them to play Saturday nights at Logan's. It helped that your dad sold Ron his first dobro guitar. Until Joe got Ron hooked on the metallic dobro sound, they'd only played instruments that originated in Appalachia."

"I should be taking notes. Did they ever play a dulcimer? I love that sound. I messed around with one today in Gatlinburg and actually managed a recognizable tune. I plan to go back to the shop and buy the one I liked best."

"You used to listen to Ron, Laurie and Zeke practice on a mandolin, banjo and either a mountain or hammered dulcimer for hours on end. After you won your first fiddling contest, they invited you to join in their jam sessions here. It was a treat for our customers."

"I want so badly to remember, Garret. I want to remember everything."

"I can help fill in some blanks, Colleen. Not now, though. I have customers to serve. Hey, I should've thought of this before. I'll phone Zeke and see if the family is in town. If they are, let's skip mass and take a run up to Pigeon Forge Sunday morning. I know they'll be happy to see you."

"We'd be back in time to meet our evening obligations, right?"

"Absolutely. Listen, I'm going to call Zeke right now. I'll phone you back ASAP."

"I'll grab my cell from my room. Call me on that." Garret hung up without giving Jo time for second thoughts.

Feeling more lighthearted than she'd ever felt before, Jo hurried to her room, put her phone in her pocket and skipped cheerfully downstairs.

"You're a happy camper," Kendra said, glancing up from the desk.

"Garret is going to try to arrange a meeting with some musicians I apparently used to know. Sunday morning if it works out. We'll be back in time for me to play here, though."

"If you need the whole day, take it."

"No, Kendra. I'm really looking forward to having a regular job. Aimless drifting isn't good for a person with memory loss. It leaves too much time to wonder and be anxious."

"Maybe that's how your mother kept you from asking too many questions—by keeping you occupied every hour of every day. Playing it looser may allow memories to start filtering back."

"Wouldn't that be nice? I confess, since I started this journey, there are times I feel close to remembering. Especially first thing in the morning. The minute I try to hone in on a particular image, bam, a curtain drops."

Jo's phone rang. "It's Garret," she whispered to Kendra, fitting the phone to her ear. "Did you talk to them? What did they say?... Are you sure you didn't badger them into it?" She laughed at his denial. "Okay, I'll be waiting on the porch at eight. Oh, Garret...I don't know about bringing my violin. If they're big recording stars now...I know you *said* we used to play together, but I don't know how to play bluegrass now." She stopped and listened intently. "Please, I'd rather just go and see them, and hear them play. I do understand your point, but... Okay, see you."

She closed her phone. "He's so stubborn. I wonder if he was like that before."

"Men always think they know best. You do what suits you, Jo. Or would you rather we call you Colleen?"

"Either, I guess. Being two people is awfully confusing, Kendra."

"It intrigues people like me, who lead boring lives. Speaking of my boring life...shall we go to the market? If we're fast, we should still have time to wander through the arts and crafts fair. Maybe you'll find a dulcimer you like without going back to Gatlinburg. I walked around the fair the day it opened. I seem to remember a booth that advertised handmade mountain instruments. Even if I'm wrong about that, I'm positive there's a booth that sells hand-churned ice cream in fresh waffle cones." Kendra licked her lips.

"You know just how to cheer me up. I'll go get my purse."

Marketing was a new experience for Jo. She realized her mother had handled that chore and the cooking while insisting Jo devote her time to her music. Pausing a minute back in the Rowans' kitchen, she reflected on everything her mother had done to keep their household running. What Jo most remembered was her mother's constant pushing. Nothing had ever quite met Sharon's approval. Not her husband, her daughter, their belongings, the circles they traveled in, Jo's career. Nothing. She realized her mother hadn't been a happy woman.

"There you go looking sad again," Kendra charged as she stored the last of the fresh vegetables they'd bought.

"I was thinking about what a complicated person my mother was. She devoted her life to me. I probably shouldn't be so angry at her."

"You have every right to be furious. Did you ask her to make you a star? In listening to your stories, I think not. You had talent, and she exploited it. Gosh, I hope that's not what I'm doing by hiring you to play for our guests."

"Heavens, no. Mother and Jerrold picked my music. You aren't. Kendra, I need to stop dwelling on them. If we're finished and if Jim doesn't need you, let's go see those arts and crafts. I'll take my car since you drove to the market. You can navigate."

The women put the rest of the groceries away and agreed to meet at Jo's car.

Kendra hurried down the steps and slid into the passenger seat. "I left Jim making up a flyer on his computer to post so guests know you'll be entertaining. I admit I told him a little white lie. I said you hoped he'd chime in on a couple of numbers because you're nervous."

"He didn't see through you?"

Kendra sighed. "God will get me, huh?"

"No. You didn't do it for selfish reasons. And strange as it may sound, I *am* nervous, Kendra. Hey, where should I park?"

They found a place not far from the fair. Tents lined several streets. Jo locked the car, and the pair began to stroll among the booths, checking out the artists' wares. Several townspeople smiled and said, "Hello, Colleen." She didn't stop to talk, but it boosted her spirits, and she returned their smiles.

Kendra bought two cookbooks. She showed Jo a recipe for shoo-fly pie. "Jim will love making these old-fashioned, down-home favorites."

"I noticed you eyeing the quilts. Why don't you go look at them while I run into the tent with the handmade instruments? It's just across the street. Shall we meet up at the end of this block in, say, twenty minutes?"

"Sounds good. Make it in front of the corner booth on your side of the street. See the tent I mean—the one with the table full of vases?"

"Gotcha." Jo struck off on her own. In the instrument tent she strummed a twelve-string mandolin, then stopped to watch a demonstration of a jaw harp. It was a flexible strip of metal attached at one end to a horseshoe-shaped wood frame. The harp produced only one sound, but the man was so skilled at manipulating his lips, cheeks and tongue on the wood while plucking the metal strip with callused fingers, he created a harmonicalike vibration that had Jo tapping her foot. Spotting a table piled with hammered and mountain dulcimers, she moved on. She particularly liked a teardrop-shaped instrument carved out of maple. The lightest stroke of her fingertips produced rich treble sounds. Determining the price fit her budget, she bought the dulcimer, and subsequently was easily talked into buying a book of music.

By then she only had five minutes left to meet Kendra. The crowd had grown, making getting to her destination more difficult. However, Jo still arrived first at the corner booth. Just past the table of vases, she spotted a pottery bowl glazed with swirls of sea-greens and aqua blues. Jo picked it up as someone farther back in the booth said, "Colleen?"

Jo turned swiftly because the voice hadn't sounded like Kendra. A tall, attractive blonde in her mid to late thirties studied Jo a minute. Jo stared back without recognition. "So, it's true. You don't know who you are," the blonde said.

"I'm sorry. Have we met?" The telltale headache that struck when she felt uncomfortable kicked in. Casting about for something to say, she was relieved to see Kendra approaching from the other side of the street.

"You look remarkably the same, Colleen. How is it you don't know me, but you had no trouble picking out your old favorite pottery piece?"

Jo quickly set the bowl down. "Who are you?"

"Sheila. Sheila Logan. Galen's wife. You spent hours watching Clare and me mix paints for Clare's signature pottery."

A second woman finished helping a customer, and wove her way through the open shelves of pots. She wore her long brown hair in a single braid. The minute her eyes lit on Jo, she squealed in delight and engulfed her in a hug. When Jo struggled, the friendly woman relaxed her grip, but said, "Colleen, it's Molly. Molly Fielding. Well, I used to be Logan. I married Matt Fielding. You remember Matt. He was in your class."

Sheila nudged her sister-in-law. "Molly, quit yammering. I believe Garret's right. Colleen's lost her mind."

A third woman with short black hair came up. "I'm Brian's wife, Kellee," she said, shaking Jo's hand.

"We've never met, but I've certainly heard your name often."

Molly hadn't totally let go of her old friend. "Kellee's family rented out summer cabins over in Sevierville. She and Brian were engaged before your family left White Oak Valley."

Sheila butted in again. "The way Joe, Sharon and you left without a word to anyone hurt our whole family. And that doesn't begin to address what your cruelty did to Garret."

"Sheila! Stop. We're overwhelming Colleen. Look how she's shaking." Molly's sparkling blue eyes filled with sympathy. "I've been so busy since I heard you were back. You'll have to forgive me. I'm still making baskets like crazy. And Matt and I have twins."

A jagged pain shot through Jo's skull. She tried to speak, but what could she say to these three women who were total strangers?

Kendra, bless her, suddenly materialized at Jo's side. "Nice pottery. We've met, I believe." She faced the women gathered around Jo, and extended a hand to Molly Fielding. "I'm Kendra Rowan. My husband, Jim, and I recently opened Buttercup Cottage as a bed-and-breakfast."

"K. Logan," Jo suddenly burst out, even as she continued to rub her forehead. "I saw a signed piece of stoneware in Gatlinburg yesterday. A silhouette of a bird in front of a red sun. Garret said it was my design." She raised her eyes to the statuesque blonde.

"Now you say this abstract watercolor was my favorite," she continued. "The thing is, I don't recall seeing either before. And I'm truly sorry for the pain I caused your family."

Molly again came to Jo's rescue. "It's okay, Colleen. Kellee and Sheila are best friends with Jaclyn Richmond and Trish Collier. Mom told me yesterday how happy Garret is to have you back. He really wants to help you remember. I hope you get better fast, so you can start weaving baskets again. Boy, could I use the help." The woman's grin reminded Jo of Garret.

Sheila sniffed. "Molly, dear, let her go. I think she has a wild look about her. I wonder if it's occurred to anyone besides Sean that maybe Colleen should still be in a mental institution."

Kendra caught the bag holding Jo's dulcimer as it slipped from her hand. Aiming a dirty look at Sheila Logan, Kendra hustled Jo to the tent's entrance. "Let's get some fresh air," she said loudly. "There's a nasty smell inside this tent."

"Great," Jo muttered as they rounded the corner. "If things weren't already strained enough between me and Garret's family, Sheila will spread rumors that I'm crazy. I should go back and—"

"And what?" Kendra asked. "Pretend you remember them? You don't, do you?"

"No. They're all strangers to me, Kendra. I ought to go home. Things, people I should know aren't familiar. It's not helping me remember."

"Rehab is like that. Two steps forward, one step back. You came here for answers. They can't all be pleasant."

"Molly was nice. And Kellee looked embarrassed. But Sheila... If she had her way I'd be on the next train back to Boston."

"Who gave her a vote?" Kendra stood aside to let Jo unlock the car. As they set their packages inside, she said, "I know I'm an outsider, but if I wrote your life as a play, you and Garret would be the main characters. Everybody else are walk-on bit players."

A smile flickered at the corners of Jo's mouth. "Will you give my play a happy ending?"

"I'm handing over Act Three to you. See that you don't screw it up," Kendra said, shaking a finger.

Their mood decidedly lighter, the women returned to the B and B. Jo spent the evening practicing a couple of semiclassical songs she planned to play for the guests Saturday night. "Greensleeves" and "Fascination" were universally recognized.

People were chitchatting and enjoying after-dinner drinks when she stood next to the piano and began performing. She warmed up with Saint-Saëns's "Danse Macabre," followed by a theme from *Cavalleria Rusticana.*

Guests set down their glasses, and the conversations stopped. Jo didn't notice; she was lost in her music.

Jim Rowan took Kendra's hand. "If she's nervous, I'm an alligator."

"She's something, huh? All the same, after a couple of these high-class tunes, this audience would probably like a piano interlude. Something pronounceable," Kendra murmured, dropping a kiss on his head.

Jim did roll up to the piano the first time Jo lifted her bow and looked around. Jim flexed his fingers and tentatively began to play "Black Magic Woman." He was pleased when after a few bars Jo began to blend her slower tempo to his chords. Jim's second song was called "I Will Remember You." Jo's eyes widened at the name on his sheet music, and Jim winked, knowing by now she could pick up and follow a tune that described her fondest wish. And so the evening went on, the two wounded musicians speaking through their music until they could play no more.

SUNDAY MORNING, Jo carried her coffee out to the porch, eagerly awaiting Garret's arrival. He wheeled into the B and B ten minutes early. His car windows were rolled down a few inches, and a dog poked a nose out the back window to sniff the air. When Garret unfolded his long body from the Suzuki and strolled toward her, Jo's heart thrummed like the dulcimer she'd been fooling around with.

"Hey, is that 'Old-Time Religion' I hear?" He set one foot on the middle step and smiled up at her.

"I'm surprised you recognized it. I need a lot of practice. Playing the violin means I've developed tougher skin on the fingers on my left hand. I'll have to get calluses on my right hand for the dulcimer. Guess what," she said, jumping up to face him with shining eyes. "Last night I played songs *I* wanted to play instead of whatever my mom and Jerrold picked."

Garret circled his arms around her waist and swung her off the ground. "That's great! You look happy today, Colleen."

He set her down and she closed the book of dulcimer music. "Is that Domino? I'm glad you brought him. Would you like a cup of coffee before we leave? Kendra made a pot of hazelnut right before I came out."

"No, I'm ready to go if you are. To be honest I wondered if you'd send me packing. I stopped at my parents' house to tell Mom I wasn't going to church this morning. Sheila and Galen were there and I heard about yesterday. I'm sorry for her comments. Even Galen said she was out of line."

"It's all right. I liked Molly and Kellee. I just wish I could remember them, Garret. Molly said we used to make baskets together. Even Sheila said I spent time watching her and your mom mix glazes. And Kellee didn't deny they'd used some of my designs."

"You were drawing a lot back then. You drew up plans for our dream house. I wanted to surprise you with the five acres I bought right before I went to Ireland."

"Oh, Garret." Jo didn't know what else to say.

He collected her book and dulcimer and put a hand

at the small of her back as they descended the steps. "I thought I wouldn't be able to build that house when it was clear you'd never share it with me. My brothers got tired of watching me mope and they forced me to buy materials. They tried to convince me to pick a different house, but I couldn't do that, Colleen."

"I'm sorry I hurt you, Garret. I'd give anything to fix that."

They reached his vehicle and he opened the door to put the dulcimer in the backseat. Domino stuck his nose out the window and sniffed the air as she shook out the full skirt of her sundress. "If it's any consolation," she said, "when I came out of the coma, I kept thinking I was stuck in a dream. I guess that sounds crazy. Maybe Sheila and Sean are right about me needing more psychiatric care."

Garret swore explosively and tipped her face up to his. He gently held her head with both hands. "Sweetheart, you are *not* crazy. Sheila, Sean and anyone else who suggests that will have to deal with me. I may be guilty of trying to force answers for you, but I swear, we're in this together. Whether or not we ever make inroads. One thing I'm sure of. You are still the gutsy woman I loved." His fingers tunneled through her curls and his thumbs stroked the soft skin of her cheeks.

She brought her right hand up to hold his wrist. "I'd be the happiest person in the world if only I could be sure of that, Garret. I'm taking baby steps here."

He laid a row of urgent kisses along her jaw to her lips. "Dammit, I want what we had, Colleen. It's hard not to want to take up where we left off."

Domino gave a hound's mournful howl as Jo slid her arms around Garret's waist. The steady beat of his heart against her ear felt right. Natural. But she held back from saying so. "You've made a life without me. No...don't deny it," she said, giving him a warning squeeze. "It's not fair for me to drop in out of nowhere and disrupt that life. We have no idea if I even deserve your love."

Garret released her slowly. "Of course you do."

"Yesterday Kendra compared my life to a play, Garret. I think Act One is a mystery. We're living Act Two. Act Three is yet to be written, and that won't happen until the scattered pieces of my past come together."

Closing his eyes, Garret dragged a hand over his face. "The hell of it is, that makes sense to me. The way I see it, the pieces are all around us." He gestured out toward the town.

"Or in Boston," she said.

"Right. Or there," Garret went around the car and climbed in the driver's seat. "We'll go there if we don't find the key here."

"No. Even though both my parents are buried up north, something in me strongly resists going back. I'll phone the hospital tomorrow."

Garret wrapped one of her red curls around his finger. "It's your call. Shall we continue on to Pigeon Forge before Domino wakes up the other guests?"

She smiled. "Every time you say Pigeon Forge I picture a giant bird feeder sitting on top of a mining forge."

Grinning, Garret started the engine. "You're in for a rude awakening. No self-respecting bird would be caught dead amid the palaces of consumerism that is Pigeon Forge."

"Really?" She shivered with excitement as Garret pulled the Suzuki out into the road and turned around.

"I'm not saying another word. I can't discount shock value in helping to restore your memory."

"Well, that's intriguing," she murmured. "Oh, good, Domino wants to share my seat." She scooted over and happily stroked the dog's soft, floppy ears.

She and Garret talked inconsequentially about the sights they passed on the five-mile drive. The dog stretched out on Colleen's lap.

"Those signs along the road advertising Dollywood. What is it?"

"Dolly Parton's theme park. It's true," Garret said when she gazed skeptically at him through gold lashes. "The holler where she grew up is just a few miles from Pigeon Forge. The town wasn't nearly as commercial then."

"Oh, so she's a former resident?"

"I understand she still spends a lot of time in the area. See, you aren't the only famous musical star from here."

Rolling her eyes, Jo turned back to the window. By

then Garret had taken the exit that led them through Pigeon Forge. "What's the big deal with miniature golf? Why so many? They're kind of gaudy," she said. "Wow, but look at the outlet stores. Do you think that's really the world's largest teddy bear store?" she asked, craning her neck to keep it in sight as Garret motored through the tourist Mecca.

"It's big. I bought you a teddy bear there once, for your sixteenth birthday. A panda about the color of Domino, but the bear's spots were bigger. You didn't care for dolls, but you had stuffed animals all over your bed."

"I did?" Her eyes grew distant, and she continued to pet the snoring dog. "The panda had a big red bow around his neck and a zipper in back that hid a place to store pajamas," she said haltingly.

Garret's foot hit the brake. He yanked off his sunglasses. "That's right. That's right! Do you still have him, is that how you know?"

She shook her head. Blinking rapidly, she rubbed her forehead. "For a second I saw a brass bed with a light blue quilt. A huge black-and-white panda sat propped against a pillow. Next to the bear was a gray cat, a brown dog, a Mickey Mouse and a...purple..."

"Unicorn," Garret shouted. "A purple unicorn I won for you by throwing baseballs at milk bottles at the county fair. You were thirteen. You'd spent all your money trying to win that gross stuffed toy. We'd split up, I can't remember why. Sean and I took off. You stayed with Molly. I had only a buck left when we met up again. You talked me into spending it on trying to win that unicorn."

"And you did, I guess," she said as she tried desperately to cling to the moment that had already faded.

"Yeah. Ten bucks later. I borrowed five from Brian and five from Galen. I had to haul trash out of the pub for a month to pay them back." He traced a finger down her freckled nose as he smiled indulgently. "See, even then you had me wrapped around your little finger."

Jo turned aside. "In Boston my bed had a plain headboard and a heavy gold bedspread. I remember that when I came home from the hospital I thought everything in the apartment smelled new. What do you suppose happened to my stuffed toys? I packed everything we owned after Mother died. The yearbooks and those few awards were in a box I think my dad stored in the closet. I doubt Mother knew they were there. I'm betting she and Jerrold got rid of possible reminders once they learned I had no memories. Jerrold managed my career. I don't know for how long."

"Thank God they missed the box with the yearbooks. Don't look so sad, Colleen. You had a memory. Sure, it was a small one, but it proves they're still in there somewhere."

"That's true." She shifted, and Domino sat up. He woofed in his throat and, as if sensing her distress, nuzzled her left ear.

"Ooh, your tongue is rough, mutt," she said, laughing. She smacked a kiss right on his wrinkled brow.

"Lucky dog," Garret said, tugging one ear before he eased into traffic again.

"Maybe I'll remember the Silverman family," she said, nestling back into the upholstery. "Are they a mother, father and son?"

"No. Husband, wife and husband's younger brother. Ron and Laurie are in their forties. Zeke's probably thirty-two or -three. He owns a banjo your dad made. And no falling for him. I used to be jealous as hell because you spent so much time with him in the back room at the pub. You both said you were practicing, but sometimes he showed up without the other two."

"I'm trying to picture you jealous. You must've had girls falling all over you."

"Nope. Well, maybe one or two who refused to believe they couldn't break us up."

She was still mulling that over when Garret pulled down a long drive that opened onto a big old house. For a fleeting moment the scene felt familiar. But the bald man, petite woman and younger lanky guy who rushed out to greet them were strangers to her. "I don't know them," she said. "But it'll be nice to meet someone else who liked my dad's work. Jerrold and my tutor in Boston said Dad's violins were amateurish. I have two. One cherrywood and one black walnut. They resonate differently. Jerrold insisted I use an Italian-made violin.

I need to return it. I'm sure it's part of the money he says he invested in me."

"I'm not musical, except for knowing what I like to listen to. I liked hearing you jam with the Silvermans in our back room while I worked the bar—no matter what kind of violin you used." Garret got out and opened Jo's door.

Jo felt overwhelmed by the enthusiastic welcome, but she accepted the Silvermans' hugs. When the greetings ended, they all retired to a wide, shady porch. Soon the clear mountain air vibrated and pulsed with soaring music. Ringing, fast-paced, foot-stomping music.

Garret fetched Jo's dulcimer, and she scrambled to keep time with the lively tunes the boisterous Silverman trio belted out. Zeke teased Jo about having lost her ability to capture the high, lonesome bluegrass wail.

She took it in stride, and her eyes sparkled. A fact Garret alluded to hours later when they said goodbye and started down the mountain.

"I loved listening to them harmonize," she said. "I learned so much about the correct way to play my dulcimer. I nearly cried when Ron brought out one of my dad's violins. Did I really used to prop a violin on my knee to play instead of resting it under my chin?" She paused. "I'm sorry, Garret. I know you hoped I'd have a breakthrough. Me, too."

"We agreed to stop apologizing for things beyond our

control. Hey, do you mind if I listen to you perform at the B and B tonight before I go to my parents' house? I know how you used to play. I want to hear what's changed."

"A lot, I suspect. You can stay if you promise not to fall asleep on me. One guest did last night. Jim had to wake him up with a ragtime piece."

Garret chuckled. "I promise not to embarrass you."

However, that turned out to be a promise he had difficulty keeping. He yawned several times before she finished playing Tchaikovsky's "Enchanted Lake" plus the *Sleeping Beauty Suite*. That, in spite of the fact that Colleen's intensity was riveting.

He grabbed her hand the minute she set her violin down. "Walk me out."

"You don't like my music," she accused, reading his silence.

"I'm sure your performance was absolutely correct for high-society Bostonians," he said, stopping to untie Domino from the tree where he'd left him. "I'd been hoping you'd come play fiddle at the pub, the way you used to do. You were dead on when you said our customers would…" He let the thought trail off.

She got the message. When he turned to kiss her, pouring all the feeling he couldn't articulate in his kiss, she broke away and gazed sadly up at him. "I'll call you tomorrow, Garret, after I talk to someone in hospital records. Tonight we both need to think about what we want from each other. Depending on what I can find out about the baby, maybe we need to reconsider if either of us has the stomach for getting any closer."

She quickly ran back into the house, not giving him the chance to speak. But she noted, as she wiped at her eyes, he didn't try. So with him it was all about her music, too.

CHAPTER NINE

THE SELECTIONS Jo had played for Garret were the most well-known of her repertoire. And he'd been bored to death. He must not understand that the music she'd chosen tonight reflected the tumultuous state of her emotions. Most of the day, he and the Silvermans had watched and waited for her to play like Colleen Drake. But she only knew how to play like Jo Carroll.

Jim intercepted her as she dashed for the stairs. "Jo, two of our guests, the Vincents from New York, cornered me at the end of your performance. They're sure we don't recognize your great talent. Mr. Vincent wrote down the name and phone number of a conductor he says could jump-start your career." Jim handed her the paper and the violin she'd left on his piano bench.

She stared blankly at the writing.

"You know we can never pay you what you're worth," Jim said.

"Right now, I'm not feeling worth very much."

"Ouch. Did Garret say something to you?"

"He wants me to be the girl I used to be. There's a huge gap between when I came into this world as Colleen Drake and when I woke up from a coma as Jo Carroll. I think I'd rather be Colleen, but what if I can't?"

"My piano instructor once said that the music we choose echoes the state of our soul. If that was true tonight, you have a restless soul."

"So true. At the moment it's restless and unhappy."

"I've been there, just going through the motions. I guess you have to ask yourself if that's how you want to spend the rest of your life."

"I already know the answer to that. Thanks, Jim." She tore up the phone number and threw the pieces in the wastebasket under the reception desk.

Once in her room, Jo got out the book of mountain tunes she'd bought with the dulcimer. She exchanged the expensive gut strings on her violin for the steel strings Ron Silverman said would turn her violin into a fiddle. *Strangs,* he called them. Zeke joked that, to him, the real difference between a violin and fiddle was that a violinist played composers like Beethoven and Bach, while a fiddler knocked out a lightning-fast "Orange Blossom Special."

Jo flattened the bridge and loved the way "Amazing Grace" sounded. She played bluegrass tunes until her arms were too tired to hold the fiddle and bow. For the first time she could remember, she thoroughly enjoyed practicing.

THE NEXT MORNING Jo slept late. The weekend guests had checked out by the time she came down for breakfast, and Kendra said it would be a full day before new arrivals showed up.

"I have some serious phone calls to make, Kendra. I'm hoping to talk to the doctors who treated me in Boston and get answers to some hard questions. I'll take my coffee and one of Jim's sausage-and-egg-filled croissants out to the porch if that's okay. I'm not sure anyone will tell me anything over the phone, but I have to try."

"That sounds like more than a single-cup-of-coffee ordeal. Give me a minute, and I'll fill one of the individual insulated carafes."

"That'll be great. Just bring it out. It's going to take me some time to find the phone numbers I need."

"We heard you playing a different kind of music after you went upstairs last night."

"Was I a bother? I tried to play softly."

"That was an observation, not a complaint. I also noticed you came downstairs humming 'Blowin' In The Wind.' Humming and smiling," Kendra said, "in spite of the stressful morning you're facing."

"I did, didn't I?" Jo scooped one of the croissants from the warming tray onto a small plate. "I've turned a corner, Kendra. I'm determined to be as upbeat as I can."

"Glad to hear it." Kendra smiled broadly as she held

open the screen door, allowing Jo to carry her plate, coffee mug and phone out to the porch.

A frustrating hour and a nearly empty coffee carafe later, Jo finally reached a resident surgeon who remembered her and was willing to chat. "This is Dr. Lim speaking. I was the head attending staff surgeon on your case, Ms. Drake. I'm sorry our records department had such a difficult time finding your chart. You were first admitted as Colleen Drake. Then your legal guardian insisted our records be changed to Jo Carroll, your professional name, for privacy's sake. Our hospital is very discreet, Ms. Carroll. We have a court document on file retroactively granting a permanent name change."

"A court document? When? I'm sorry, I don't remember back beyond the day I emerged from the coma. That's why I have so many questions."

"The date on the name-change document is June 25. That's two weeks after you came out of the coma." Jo wrote down that date.

"Dr. Lim, is there any record of me being pregnant at the time of the accident?"

She heard him thumbing through pages.

"I see a note in the records that came up to the surgical floor with you from the emergency room. You apparently suffered a spontaneous abortion, er, miscarriage in the ambulance. Spontaneous abortion is the medical term for when the miscarriage happens in the early stages of pregnancy and is without complications. Our trauma team estimated that you were approximately twelve to thirteen weeks gestation. That's still fairly early in a pregnancy. It's not surprising you aborted considering the amount of abdominal trauma you sustained in the accident."

She couldn't help the tears that filled her eyes. Snuffling, Jo tried to hold the phone and blot them away.

She heard more rapid riffling of pages, then the doctor said briskly, "I assume you want to know if we found any abnormalities that could rule out future pregnancies. I see nothing. We removed your spleen and repaired a tear in the colon that caused you to bleed internally after the initial surgery. You developed a rather persistent infection. Eventually that was conquered. All in all, you were discharged a healthy young woman."

"Except for continued loss of long-term memory. I didn't know any of this, Dr. Lim. Not even about the pregnancy," she said.

"Really? I see a number of references that our staff doctors met with your mother, who is listed as your only next of kin."

"At eighteen wouldn't I have been responsible for myself?" Jo let the breeze dry her wet cheeks and struggled to clear her throat. She wanted the doctor to take her seriously.

"If your admission had been routine, yes, you would've been making legal decisions. But your case was far from routine. Are you aware the first paramedics on the scene listed you as deceased? You were revived en route to our facility, and spent two hours in our emergency room before anyone could reach your next of kin. A note says your mother had been summoned to the coroner's office to identify your father. You remained unconscious, so it's understandable that Mrs. Drake became your guardian of record. She authorized your surgeries. We are a first-responder trauma center, and we do our very best here," he said sternly.

"Yes. I'm not calling to blame anyone, Doctor. My parents are both gone now, and I'm trying to make sense of things I was told after the accident but now I find aren't true. I know I saw a psychologist. I'd like to speak with her if I can."

"I presume you mean Dr. Robillard. She made two entries on your record. Uh, I see she was dismissed by your mother. Dr. Robillard thought it was premature. Under these circumstances, I'm reluctant to give you her phone number. Tell you what, if you give me a number where you can be reached, I'll have her contact you if she feels she has anything to add. As far as our records go, you're entitled to see them in their entirety under the Patient Open Information Act. Or we can send a photocopy out to your current physician, providing you mail or fax us a signed authorization."

"I don't know where I'll be settling permanently, but I'll keep that in mind. I'll give you my cell number to pass on to Dr. Robillard. I hope she'll agree to speak with me. Maybe my mother said something to her that might help. I'm hoping for a miracle, I know, but…"

"We try to be in the miracle worker business. Good luck, Ms. Drake."

Jo closed her phone thoughtfully. She'd had no idea her mother had legally changed her name without even consulting her. Was it possible to change it back? Would a judge believe she hated feeling like two people? *And the baby.* There had been a baby after all.

Covering her face with her hands, Jo couldn't contain the sobs that erupted when she thought about the baby—her baby—who'd never had a chance.

A shadow fell across the table, blocking the sun.

She lifted her head, not knowing how she could explain her obvious distress to a stranger. Garret gazed down on her, his face awash in uncertainty.

Jo launched herself out of the wicker chair and into his arms, seeking solace, not caring when the cell phone clattered to the ground. "I just spoke with one of the doctors in Boston. He…he confirmed I lost the baby. Our baby, Garret. It hurts so bad to think no one told me." Her body shook from the wrenching sobs.

Garret held her tight against his chest and murmured into the damp curls sticking to her cheek. "I was at work. During a break I tried to call your cell several times. When it was always busy, I phoned the B and B. Kendra said you'd come outside to phone the hospital. I was afraid…I knew…honey, I just wanted to be here if you needed me."

Struggling for control, she came down off her tiptoes, but kept her face pressed against the front of his shirt. "I'll bet your brothers aren't pleased."

"They'll get over it. Will you?"

Her hands slid down to finger his shirt buttons. "Our child ought to be starting first grade next fall, Garret. The doctor said I lost the baby on the way to the hospital. I have to presume Mother knew. It was right there in the chart, yet no one told me." Her voice broke again.

"I grieved for you and our baby a long time ago. You need to give yourself time to mourn now, Colleen."

She leaned back and stared at him through misty eyes. "That's another thing. My mother petitioned to have my name legally changed to Jo Carroll after I emerged from the coma. She said it was for professional privacy. I figure that was Jerrold's suggestion. His neighbor was a judge, and a huge sponsor of the orchestra. Mother should've had my permission. I want my name back, Garret. Maybe it's silly, but I need to feel like I'm Colleen Drake again. I'm not sure of a lot, but I know I wasn't happy living in Boston as Jo Carroll."

"It's not silly. You'll need to write away for your original birth certificate. I suppose you'll also need a copy of the name-change order. Once you have those, we'll go to the county courthouse and you can file for a reversal. I'll be a witness if you need one."

She brushed a kiss across his chin. He bent to give her better access to his lips. It was a desperate kiss, but one cut short prematurely when Jo's cell phone rang.

He kept one arm around her and leaned down to pick it up.

She checked the display. "It's a Boston area code. I left my number for the psychologist," she said. "She may not be able to tell me any more than the surgeon did, but I need to ask her." Shaking back her hair, Jo answered the call on the third ring. "Dr. Robillard, I'm glad you called. I didn't know if you'd even remember me."

"Do you want me to stay?" Garret mouthed.

"No," she murmured. "Go on back to work. I'll stop at the pub if I find out anything helpful," she said, cupping her hand over the phone.

Clearly hating to go off and leave her, he trailed a hand over her hair and down her arm. But she needed to concentrate on the conversation, so Garret left her and jogged off to his Grand Vitara.

"I realize I didn't have much to say to you when you came into my hospital room, Dr. Robillard. The world wasn't making sense to me at the time. Much of it still isn't."

"Ms. Drake, you should see a therapist even now. I understand your memory hasn't returned."

"No. Maybe it's not ethical for you to discuss any interactions you had with my mother, but she passed away suddenly two months ago. After her death, I discovered that she'd concocted a false background and fed me a pack of lies. Now I'm trying to learn more of the truth and put my life back together."

"Mrs. Drake ordered me off your case. At first she tried to simply refuse to let you be treated, but the hospital balked. Then one day she dropped by my office and said if I didn't voluntarily withdraw she would make my professional life hell by making allegations of negligence and malpractice. She wasn't going to let anything interfere with your musical career. I had to weigh my value to one patient against the help I hoped to provide many. That said, I did meet with your medical team and said that in my professional opinion you needed follow-up psychological care. I was equally sure your mother wouldn't allow it. How shall I put this...she was a forcefully charming woman on the surface."

"That's a good description. Still, I was her daughter. What would possess her to make up such elaborate stories all for the sake of furthering a career?"

"I wouldn't butt into this if she was alive. You should try to forget about why. Your mother was very troubled. It's all clear in some of the remarks she made to nurses and doctors who handled your case. I pieced a lot together. You were an accident. She had no intention of marrying your father or anyone. In those days, the music barons dictated the morality of especially their female singers. Hard to believe, given what's in the news today. But it was a different world then. She got married but still lost the record deal that had been in the works. She wasn't able to break in again after you were born. By the time you were three, you were already showing promise as a violinist. The afternoon she ranted at me, I surmised much of her anger centered on revenge on the pop music industry. Your father may have been able to rein her in had he lived. When I met Sharon she had sole control of your future."

"I had no idea. But everything you've said gels with what I've learned here in White Oak Valley. I should pity her, I suppose."

"If you can, and can let go of your own anger, I think you'll be a step closer to recovery."

"You've been very kind to take so much time with me. Let me give you the address here so that you can send me a bill for consultation."

"Thank you for offering, but there's no need. Now I can release some of my own guilt. I felt I should've tried to do more. Gone up the chain, maybe, to the chief administrator. My excuse is that he's known for always taking a patient's side against his staff."

"My mother had influential allies." Jo thought about Jerrold and his neighbor, the judge who'd undoubtedly helped facilitate the name change.

"I don't mean to cut you off, but my receptionist says my next appointment has arrived."

"Please, don't let me keep you. I appreciate how candid you've been."

"I wish you luck scaling the barriers of dissociative fugue. I sense you're where people want to see you get well. My advice, and I believe it's one thing I managed to tell you in the hospital, is don't try to force the memories. It's better if you're able to relax and immerse yourself in love and support."

Garret immediately came to mind. "Thank you. I'll try to keep that in mind. Goodbye, and thanks again." As Jo disconnected, she saw that her battery was low. She was debating running back upstairs to charge it before going to the pub, when her phone rang again.

"Hi," he said. "I was getting worried because your line was busy so long. I was nervous for you. Are you okay?"

"I am. Really okay. I have a lot to tell you. I wish I'd contacted Dr. Robillard before now. But, Garret, I'm losing my cell battery. I thought I might drive down to the pub."

"You could, except Brian and Sean just got through saying I'm worthless and I should take the rest of the day off to get my act together. How about if I swing by and pick you up? I'll take you to our hideaway. It's warm enough for a dip under the waterfall, so dig out your bathing suit. As long as you're feeling up to an outing."

"I am. It's just what the doctor ordered. She said relaxing will help more than forcing my brain to try to remember. Do I have time to see if Jim can make us a picnic? Lunch by a waterfall sounds very relaxing."

Garret laughed. "You used to pack a hamper whenever we went there. And I'm always first in line to eat. I want this day to be yours, Colleen. Let me go by the house and make sure Domino has enough water for the afternoon and into the evening in case we stay to watch the moon come up. If I'm there in half an hour, will you have enough time to get ready?"

"That's perfect. Bye, Garret."

She all but skipped inside. Kendra glanced up from dusting in the living room. "Hey, look at you. You must've had good news."

"I'd tell you how good, but Garret invited me on a picnic. I need to bring the lunch, though. Well, it was my idea," she admitted. "If Jim's not around, I'll make sandwiches and take apples we picked from your orchard. You can put an extra food charge on my bill. I have to run up to my room to grab a sweater and plug my cell into the charger. Oh, Garret said to bring a swimsuit. I don't have one, Kendra. I don't even know if I can swim."

Kendra wiggled her eyebrows. "You can always go skinny-dipping."

"Skinny-dip…ohh, that's too daring for me."

"You never know, maybe the old you was more adventurous. I love picnics," Kendra added, sighing. "Please, let me make the lunch. Picnic surprises add to the pleasure. Do yourself a favor…when you get upstairs take a look in the mirror. You have more color in your cheeks than I've seen since you got here."

"I just went through a real emotional roller coaster during my two phone calls. I came away more optimistic. I should probably tone it down a couple of notches. Maybe nothing will change after all."

"There's no such thing as too much optimism. Now shoo, let's get this show on the road." Kendra motioned her friend up the stairs with a swish of her feather duster.

It was only after Jo entered her room that she realized she felt like a new woman. A woman named Colleen. She used the time Kendra gave her to experiment with a new hairstyle she'd admired in one of Kendra's women's magazines. Her wardrobe wasn't exciting. A few plain, dark-colored dresses and slacks. Her mother's dictates.

Her mother had pitched a fit when Jo bought two pairs of jeans with her first check from the coffeehouse. But after talking to Dr. Robillard, Jo felt she had permission to slam the door on Sharon's rigid rules.

It felt good—sexy—to tie up one side of a too-big, blue T-shirt, exposing a narrow strip of her belly.

"Wow," Kendra said, then whistled when Jo bounded into the kitchen to collect the lunch. "I hope Garret has a lot of willpower."

They heard him drive up, sparing Jo the need to answer.

Garret had the same reaction as Kendra. "Wow," he said as he rushed around the SUV to open the passenger door. "You look…great," he said. "Really great!"

His eyes swept her from head to toe and lingered on her bare midriff. Belatedly he relieved her of the basket Kendra had covered with jaunty red-plaid napkins.

Accepting her new power, the woman who now tried to think of herself as Colleen turned to face Garret after they were both buckled in. "You mentioned swimsuits. I don't own one. You'll have to tell me if I used to know how to swim."

"As kids we spent most of the summer in the creek. The state tightened park rules when we were in high school, but locals felt the rules applied only to visitors to the Smoky Mountains. If no one has found our private waterfall, you can take a dip wearing just your underwear." He couldn't help his eager masculine grin.

"Maybe I'll do that," she said, surprising her companion. Pleasantly surprising him, she could tell from his seductive, sidelong glances. He immediately settled back for the drive and began whistling a tune she couldn't name.

Eventually he slid a CD into the car player and lively bluegrass tunes replaced his whistling.

She found herself mentally attempting to follow along with her violin. She didn't realize she'd begun to move her fingers as if she was playing, until Garret commented on it.

"Even if I don't remember having played bluegrass before, I think I could easily become a convert. It has a lonesome, Celtic sound that appeals to me."

He nodded in time to the beat, and tapped his hands on the steering wheel. They were both feeling the exuberance sparked by the music, sunshine flickering through the trees, and of having an afternoon together.

Garret turned off onto a dirt road. Branches scraped the top of the Vitara, and he slowed markedly.

"I would've missed this road completely if I'd been the one driving."

"It's a fire road. I wasn't sure it'd still be open. I haven't been up here in years. Not since the afternoon right before I went to Ireland."

"You didn't bring, uh…Jackie here?" she asked, but avoided meeting his eyes.

"You don't get it yet, do you? This is our *special* place, Colleen," he said, stressing the special part.

"Okay, fine, Garret. Let's not spoil the day bickering." She stretched her arms up as if to hug the moment.

He drove on without speaking. The road had narrowed to little more than twin tracks, and it took all his concentration to follow it through the thick underbrush.

She knew when they'd arrived. Not because she remembered the spot, but because the Suzuki burst out of the thicket into a glade. "It's as if we're on top of the world," she exclaimed.

"You always said that," he told her, pulling on the hand brake.

Suddenly self-conscious under the intensity of his probing gaze, she released her seat belt and cracked open her door. "Oh, listen. Hear the waterfall. And the birds are singing. I want to go see. Shall I take the lunch, or do we want to come for it later?"

"I brought a blanket to spread out on the ground. You run on. I'll get it from the trunk and collect the lunch basket."

Colleen took him at his word. She had such hopes that her first glimpse of an area that meant so much to them would instantly unlock her memories. She felt subtly comforted by the scene, but no more than what she'd felt the day she stood at the overlook and stared out at the great Smoky Mountains.

"It's beautiful," she said, sensing Garret come up behind her. "But I don't remember ever being here before."

"Don't sweat it, Colleen. Enjoy this moment by moment." He pointed to a level spot about fifty yards from the waterfall. "Let's spread the blanket there. We can see the sun make rainbows in the spray, but we'll be far enough back that we won't get wet."

"I'll help," she volunteered, and immediately picked her way across rock and fallen trees.

Garret set the basket aside and flipped the folded blanket so she could grasp two corners of it. He bent to straighten his half, and a gold chain fell out of the open neck of his shirt.

She reached out and caught the oak-leaf pendant in her fingers. "This is the necklace you ripped off me my second day in town. The day Jerrold tried to get me to go back to Boston." Confusion filled her eyes.

Closing one hand over hers, Garret pressed a finger of his other hand over her trembling lips. "No. Give me a minute. I had your necklace repaired." Releasing her, he pulled a matching necklace out of his pocket. They were identical, except that the second chain was daintier than the one he wore.

Dropping to his knees on the blanket, he tugged her down beside him and fastened the chain around her neck. "I gave this to you the day we came here and made plans to get married. You brought the designs for our house. The one I said I'd build for us. That was the day we made love and you got pregnant." He traced a finger near her wide eyes.

"You gave me the matching one here the day before I left for Ireland with my mom. You said you'd found out the oak leaf stood for loyalty, and that if we both wore them always, we'd be bound no matter how many miles separated us. We'd always return to each other." Breathless, he added softly, "And we have, Colleen. We have."

Their lips moved closer until a kiss was inevitable.

Birds trilled and the waterfall thundered. Love swelled in Colleen's heart as their kisses intensified and they lay down together on the blanket. The sun warmed their already overheated skin. Garret was first to strip off his shirt.

She kissed the hollow of his neck. Easing up on one elbow, she turned his oak leaf over. There was an inscription: *I will never leave you.* Below that, her real name, *Colleen.*

"I left you, Garret. I made a promise and broke it. Is that why your family is so upset with me? Is that why Mildred said I owed you a huge apology? Did none of them ever break promises they made as teenagers? This had to have been before I graduated, Garret."

"You didn't graduate. At least not from White Oak High. I told my mom I had to be back for your ceremony. I insisted. When we got home the week of graduation, you were gone."

She stroked his tanned skin, and the dusting of hair swirled around his nipples. "That explains why there was no picture of me in a cap and gown in the last yearbook." Dropping her hand, she pressed her flat stomach. "How pregnant would I have been at graduation? Would everyone have seen?"

"We wouldn't have cared," he said, sliding his hands up under her T-shirt. "We fell in love hard your sophomore year. I was a senior. My folks considered you another daughter. Maybe things would've turned out different if Dad had gone with Mom instead of me. He doesn't like to fly. But when Mom insisted she was going to her family reunion that spring, he didn't want her to travel alone. Since I was the last Logan to go to work at the pub I was nominated."

"My mother was so happy you were going away," she said slowly, as a faint glimmer of that time filtered back.

"You've got that right," he said, pillowing her red curls on his arm. "I counted every week, day, hour and minute we were apart. My stomach sank when we got back and no one answered your door. Then Dad remembered that you'd left me a note. I was so relieved. All hell broke loose the day Harvey Bolton put the For Sale sign up in your front yard. He told us about your accident, and it was like someone cut out my heart, Colleen."

Lifting her head, she kissed him. "We used to sneak out of choir practice and hide behind the church, stealing kisses. I hung on your neck while you carved our initials into the base of the footbridge. You and Sean, or sometimes just you, used to drive me to the bluegrass festival. I always won in my age group. Mom hated that Dad paid my entry fees." Colleen rolled to face Garret. "I remember. I remember that. Garret, did I stand on the bar at your pub and fiddle my head off? I can hear people clapping and see them laughing. Oh, and once you came out of the kitchen and passed around sizzling burgers. Then you jumped up beside me. I was so into my song, you scared me half to death. But we danced—oh, how we danced—and people loved it."

"And afterward we slipped away and drove here. Do you remember that night, Colleen?"

She grabbed on to him. "No, no. That's all I have. Tell me about the rest of that night, Garret."

He dragged a hand down his face. "I was foolish, because I came here totally unprepared to make love with you. That's the night you got pregnant. It just…happened.

The night was magic. We were in love, Colleen. I've never stopped loving you. Do you believe that?"

"I want to believe. I want to remember more. I want to experience everything, Garret. Help me find that magic." She sat up and shrugged out of her T-shirt, offering everything she had to give.

"I want that, too," he said shakily. "This is where we made love the first and last times. Tell me again that you're sure you want to take up from where we left off. I promise I didn't bring you here to rush you. But today I am prepared…to give you all my love if you'll have it." He ran a finger down her cheek and over her lips. His eyes held hers.

"I'm sure," she whispered. "Yes, I'm sure." *She wanted to be.*

CHAPTER TEN

GARRET HAD EVERY INTENTION of going slowly. Nothing had been as important to him in a very long time. This time was all about pleasing Colleen. He'd forgotten that she never did anything in half measures. Even on the brink of womanhood she hadn't been a passive lover. Nothing had changed since then.

As her sun-warmed skin heated under Garret's exploring fingers, she flared, sending him to the brink, as well. But then his fingers slid over the puckered scars that marked her abdomen. At once he sat up to better see what he'd encountered. There were two uneven scars. One vertical, one horizontal. Both made him hurt for the pain they must've caused her.

"Garret, what's wrong?" she asked, confused and hurt by the abrupt change.

"I was about to ask you that. Damn, Colleen, what did they do to you in Boston? Are you okay? Should we be, uh, doing this?"

"They're ugly, I know." She tried to cover them with her hands. "I have worse. A wide one inside my left thigh. I broke my femur in the accident and the bone poked through my skin." She attempted to escape his eyes—his obvious horror. But he held her tight.

"While you're examining me, here's one you missed." She turned, giving him a view of her hip. "That's where they took skin for a graft after one site on my belly became infected. And don't forget about the scar on my head." With shaky motions, she shoved aside her bangs to expose the thin white line she'd shown him before. "I understand they're not pretty. No wonder you don't want to touch me."

He grabbed her hands and pulled them to his lips. "Stop it. I'm worried about you, that's all." He bent over and ran kisses along the horizontal scar on her belly. "The last thing I'd ever want to do, Colleen, is bring you more pain." His anguish showed on his face.

"It's okay, Garret," she said softly. "Those injuries healed years ago. I have occasional headaches that come when I push myself to try to remember. But earlier, when I talked to the surgeon, he assumed I'd phoned and asked about losing the baby because I was afraid I might not be able to have any more children. He said I wouldn't have any problems."

"So you're...okay to make love?"

She dipped her head and blushed. "If I haven't forgotten how." Turning her face away, she tucked her head under Garret's chin. And felt a surge as his body came to life.

"You were doing fine at everything before I went

cold on you," he said, his voice gravelly. "I think I'm back on track if you are."

It only took a few deep, stimulating kisses for Colleen to fall under his spell again.

He'd held his sexual appetite in check for all the years he'd mourned her, but now lit by her sweet passion, it burned hot and fast. Too fast. The explosion came too soon to curb Garret's desire. Colleen sagged against him, spent, but probably not fully satisfied, either.

Garret gathered her in his arms, and carried her to the cool pond at the base of the waterfall.

"Eek, it's freezing," she squealed, climbing his body. "Don't drop me. What if I can't remember how to swim?"

"I won't let go. Give it a minute. We'll warm up together," he promised, kissing her over and over.

He wasn't kidding. Hanging on to Garret's shoulders, and gripping his hips with her thighs, it wasn't long at all before Colleen was caught up in him and the rainbow prisms in the spray around them. She reveled in the gentle clink of their matching gold oak-leaf pendants—the only thing either of them wore.

This time their lovemaking was slow, easy and sustained. They peaked together, but when Colleen flew apart she felt absorbed by the brightly colored droplets raining over them.

Garret carried her to the shallows and eventually fell with her on the blanket. Curled into his side, Colleen was content to have him rub away her goose bumps, and hold her in his arms until the sun dried them. Very soon they both closed their eyes and drifted into sleep.

When Colleen came slowly awake, Garret was sitting up, tugging on his jeans. She smiled and stifled a carefree yawn. Leaning up on one elbow, she said with a happy sigh, "Logan's Cade is the most beautiful spot on earth. I wish we could stay here forever."

His hands stilled as he buckled his belt. "What did you call this place?"

Sitting up, Colleen frowned and reached for her own clothes. Sliding her panties over her hips, she shook hair out of her eyes. Her careful knot had come loose with their earlier exertions. "We called our hideaway Logan's Cade, because technically this hidden valley is on your parents' land."

"Yes," he said, excitement growing as he fell to his knees. "We named it one day in your junior year when we managed to ditch Sean and Molly and sneak off by ourselves in the old beater car I drove then," he said.

She caught his excitement. "I was supposed to be studying for a Tennessee history class. You thought one test question would be the fact the town was named by a Northerner. You said a Tennessee native would've called it White Oak Cade, since that's the Southern term for valley."

"You said technically it ought to be Logan's Grotto for the cave behind the falls."

"We argued all the way home, Garret. But we still

agreed it'd be our special place. No matter what we called it, we wouldn't share it with anyone." She crumpled her shirt between her hands. "How can I know that?"

Garret looked unsure. But joy was mounting in her as she dived excitedly into her shirt, while willing memories of her childhood to come back. Suddenly they did. She saw herself blowing out five candles on a chocolate birthday cake. And remembered the brick school she'd attended in Los Angeles that had palm trees flanking the walkway. She remembered coming home from third grade to find her mother in tears, and her father saying they were moving to White Oak Valley, Tennessee, because he'd found a supply of hardwood to make his instruments. Sharon Drake had rarely smiled after that. But Colleen had instantly fallen in love with the rambling old house, the town and…their next-door neighbors. The memories began blurring together. Some were bright and clear, some subdued as all the years she thought she'd never get back, rolled through her head like a movie.

Her hand flew to her mouth. "The accident. Garret, I remember the accident—and what came before it." She started to shake, and Garret made her stop and take a deep breath. He draped her cardigan around her shoulders, and held her in his arms. "Take it easy," he murmured. "Tell me about it if you want to. Or keep it to yourself."

"What if it all disappears again? I want to tell you."

Nodding, he snuggled her against his side and held her hand.

"I remember you'd been gone two days when my mother announced we were going to Boston. We'd been arguing for weeks because she made me practice, practice, practice nothing but classical music. I didn't want to go to Boston, and she wouldn't tell me why I had to. Dad said she'd arranged for me to play for a violin instructor who might come to Tennessee to tutor me if I was good enough. It turned out not a word of that was true." She clutched Garret's arm.

"Your dad played a part? That surprises me. He always seemed easygoing. He didn't discipline you the way my dad did us."

"Dad didn't say much on the trip. I remember asking why Mom had packed so many suitcases for such a short trip. They just looked at each other and wouldn't answer me." She paused to rub her temples.

"Don't say any more if it's too painful," Garret said, kissing her forehead.

"I want to. My appointment was at two o'clock the day we got to Boston. We met with a teacher at Boston Conservatory. Actually there were three men there to hear me play. My parents said they were going to check in to our hotel, so they left. I played until four o'clock. The men all seemed pleased by my performance. Dad came alone to pick me up. He and the men went into an office to talk while I cased my violin. He was in there so long I went to wait for him in the car. He seemed distracted when he came out. And he drove us, not to a hotel, but to an apartment."

"Did you ask why?"

"Yes. Mother said it was a residence hotel and the rent was cheaper. I was still in bed the next morning when the phone rang. I heard my name, and heard Mother tell Dad to find a pen to write down the times I'd be going to classes every day."

Colleen laid her head on Garret's shoulder. "I dressed and demanded to know what they were talking about. Mother grabbed me hard by my shoulders. She said we weren't ever going back to White Oak Valley. I'd been accepted to the Boston Conservatory, and didn't I understand how lucky I was? I missed everything she said after that. I yelled, 'No, I'm not staying.' Dad looked upset but said it was a done deal. He said he'd been responsible for the collapse of my mother's career. I think he said Mother and I would stay in Boston and he'd go sell our home here."

"Stop, Colleen. You're crying." Garret tried to wipe away her silent tears. "You don't need to say more, honey."

"I do. I need to tell you, Garret. I blurted out then and there that I was pregnant. I told them that as soon as you got back from Ireland, and after I graduated, we were getting married." Colleen's fingers inched up and covered her cheek. "Mother slapped me. I was hysterical. I remember grabbing Dad's car keys off the counter, and shouting that I was going home. I ran out

and down a ton of stairs. The car was in the basement.
I got in and was crying so hard I almost couldn't get it
started. There was a Stop sign at street level. I
should've locked the passenger door, but I didn't think
of it. Dad caught up to me there and got in the passenger seat. I drove off anyway. He tried reasoning with
me. I said no again. By then we were both crying.
Garret, do you remember how our old Buick tended to
cut out? We were barely out of Boston when it did that.
I didn't even know I was stalled on train tracks until
Dad unbuckled his seat belt and screamed at me to get
out. He grabbed me, pleading. He said mother wanted
more for me than to be stuck in Tennessee. I said I'd
teach music when Mr. Rice retired. There must've been
bells or lights or something, but I didn't see the train
barreling toward us. I don't believe Dad did, either."

Garret pressed her face into his shirt and rocked her.

"Dad tried to open my door. It was jammed. I heard
the train's horn blowing over and over. There was a
horrible squeal and sound of ripping metal. The next
thing I remember, I woke up in the hospital. I hurt
everywhere. Different people, including Mother, kept
asking what happened at the tracks. I couldn't
remember, and the more they asked, the more I
panicked. I blacked out again. That time when I woke
up, nurses and doctors told me how many surgeries I'd
had, and that I'd been in a coma for two weeks.
Garret…that accident was my fault. I caused Daddy's
death." Colleen started to shake uncontrollably.

Garret dragged her onto his lap. "Sweetheart, you can't undo the past. And you have to know, Colleen, your parents are partly to blame. Think about what they did."

"Mother was, certainly. And by losing my memory, I made everything that much easier. Jerrold Cleary showed up at the hospital a week after I came out of the coma. After someone decided to see if I could still play the violin."

"And you could. That really was a miracle, Colleen."

"I guess. But now I know Jerrold was one of the three men who listened to my audition. Mother introduced him to me as my manager. Jerrold pulled up a chair and started talking about when I'd be able to go back and play with the orchestra…as though I'd been a member before the accident. I believe that's when everyone started calling me Jo Carroll. Oh, between them, Mother and Jerrold had logical answers to all my questions." She pressed her tear-streaked cheek into Garret's still-naked shoulder and wept harder.

Not knowing what else to do, he tightened his hold and let her cry until she had no more tears, only great gulping hiccups.

"The sun's going down," she said when she finally stirred. "You should put on a shirt, Garret. You'll get cold."

"I'm fine. All I care about is that you're okay."

She slid off his lap and put on her sandals.

Garret shrugged into his T-shirt and put on his boots

before Colleen broke the silence. "The way I see it, my mother and father sacrificed everything so that I would be a classical violinist. The afternoon you and I walked in Jim and Kendra's orchard, I said maybe I should go back to Boston and rejoin the orchestra. I feel more pressure to do that now."

"I reminded you then that you told Jerrold playing with the orchestra bored you. Shouldn't you give yourself more time to adjust, Colleen? Will spending your life doing something you don't like atone for Joe's death? Your dad took you to Boston because he thought he'd wronged your mom. Sharon manipulated you both."

Colleen picked at her fingernail and stared out at the setting sun. "I don't know why you don't hate me for not keeping our secret about the baby the way we agreed. If I hadn't blown up, if I'd bided my time and called you after you got back from Ireland, Garret, you would've come for me. There wouldn't have been an accident."

He wrapped one of her curls around his forefinger. "That wouldn't be like you, Red. You always stood up for yourself."

Turning, she gazed at him. "I remember a lot of things now, Garret. You and I used to argue for the sake of arguing."

"Nah, we argued for the sake of making up," he teased. "I'll bet you can't remember a single time I walked away and didn't come back for more, can you?"

She shook her head. "Seven years is a long time, though. Where *do* we go from here?"

"For starters we can see what you brought in that lunch basket. I'm suddenly starving."

"In a minute it'll be too dark to see what Kendra sent. She wanted to make the lunch, so I let her."

"I have a gas lantern in the trunk. If you unload the basket, I'll get it."

She hesitated a minute, then relented, "I'm hungry, too. I can't believe I feel so normal, considering an hour ago I still didn't have a memory. Then I woke up from a catnap and all those missing years flooded back."

"Would it sound like bragging if I said you were rag-doll relaxed after we made love that second time under the waterfall? We probably steamed through any barriers."

She tossed a pinecone at him, and all of a sudden it felt as though they'd never been apart.

He dodged it neatly, flashed a cheeky grin and trotted off.

Colleen sank down on the blanket, but instead of digging straight into the lunch basket, she savored the thrill of watching Garret's athletic body—a body she knew intimately.

She gave herself a little shake and reached for the basket, removing the lid. Kendra had outdone herself. She'd packed sandwiches, both egg and chicken salad. And two red apples. Wedged into one side, a bottle of white wine and two glasses. Not plastic ones, but real glass.

Garret would be back soon with his lantern, but Colleen found Kendra had included a pair of cut-glass hurricane lamps and candles. Next she pulled out a linen tablecloth and two snowy napkins. Kendra had thought of everything for a romantic picnic—even matches to light the candles.

Smiling to herself, Colleen spread the tablecloth. She had the candles lit by the time Garret arrived.

"You didn't tell me you'd planned a romantic candlelight dinner," he said, setting the lantern down off the blanket as he sat cross-legged next to Colleen.

"Thank Kendra for all of this." Colleen waved a hand over the goodies. "She even thought of a corkscrew. I'll let you do the honors." She passed him the bottle. "Shall I split the sandwiches so we have half of each kind?"

"Tonight, princess, your slightest wish is my command," Garret said, removing the cork with a soft pop. "You'll have to tell me if this is good. You know I'm a beer kinda guy." He poured an inch of wine into one glass and handed it to Colleen.

"We didn't have liquor at our apartment. Before we moved to Boston I wasn't old enough to drink." She studied the pale liquid.

"Only sarsaparilla, but you know that."

"I know what it looked like, Garret, but that wasn't a memory. I was as shocked as you were." She studied her glass. "I really can't tell good wine from bad."

"Then we'll test this together." Holding out the bottle, Garret filled both their glasses, then raised his. "A toast to us," he said, touching the rim of his glass to hers with a musical ping. Garret started to drink, then hesitated. Colleen was twirling her glass, gazing at him nervously.

"To us? What does that mean exactly, Garret? Earlier you said we were picking up where we left off seven years ago, but…"

"You have doubts?"

"Back then we were ready to get married." The hand not clutching her glass twisted the oak-leaf pendant hanging from her neck.

He set his glass on the closed top of the picnic basket. "I'm not suggesting we run straight to the altar if you want to wait, sweetheart."

She sipped her wine to buy some time before answering. "Even now that I've remembered, we both know your life continued on while mine was on hold."

"My life was pretty much on hold, too. My feelings for you haven't changed, Colleen. I think I proved that today."

She averted her eyes from the emotion in his eyes and the shadow of a beard that left him looking slightly dangerous. Instead she studied the swift-rising moon.

"I realize our future depends on if you're willing to stay in White Oak Valley," he said, tightly gripping his glass.

She said nothing but opened the sandwiches and passed him a plate.

"Say something. You've cut your ties to Boston. I have a stake in the pub, and a house and land here."

"You said I designed the house. I vaguely remember that, and sketching patterns for your mother's pottery." Taking a bite of egg salad, she chewed thoughtfully. "I could go somewhere brand-new, and start my life fresh."

"I want you to stay." Garret set his plate down and reached across the candles to trace her jaw.

She felt the pull of their history, hidden from her for so long behind a web of lies. Snippets of happier times living in White Oak Valley had begun filtering through. "Whatever I resurrect here, Garret, I'm sure will make me happier than I've been. I've always wanted a husband and family of my own one day. Mother was quick to tell me such dreams were meaningless. Maybe I will stay. And give us a try."

Leaning forward, he pressed a tender kiss to her lips. "You taste like egg salad."

"You dope." She swatted at his broad shoulders. The playful exchange made them both laugh. They took their time enjoying the simple meal. Finally Colleen stowed the remnants, and Garret corked the wine. They moved closer together and sat with his head cradled on Colleen's lap, watching the moonlight dance across the water.

"It's getting late. We probably should head back," he said, yawning. "Will you come home with me? I want you to see how the house turned out."

"Can I take a rain check?" She smoothed her fingers over a lock of hair that fell stubbornly over his forehead. "I'm pretty beat. I want to be at my best when I tour your home for the first time."

He pushed himself to his feet, offering her a hand. "I'd hoped I could talk you into spending the night," he said lightly. "I don't mean to rush you. It's just…we've lost so much time already. And I've been neglecting work. I know because Brian and Sean remind me every five minutes." He screwed up his face as he collected the lantern and picnic basket and stepped aside to allow Colleen room to fold the blanket.

They fell into step. "Jim and Kendra are paying me a little to help clean rooms and play violin on weekends. It doesn't cover my cost to stay there, so I need to make some plans. Either find a job or a cheaper place to live."

"You can stay with me for free," he said, stowing the picnic stuff in the compact trunk.

"Don't take this wrong, Garret, but I've been dependent too long. I need to see if I can make it on my own."

He didn't speak while they settled themselves in the car. Before starting the engine, he said, "One thing I want to be clear, we have to speak our minds to each other, Colleen. We always did. Yeah, we argued, but if we can be open, feelings won't get and stay hurt."

"Agreed."

"Another thing," he added once they were underway, "My family has always known you're the woman I love. I want them to start seeing us together again. Tomorrow night, come hang out at the pub. It's catfish Tuesday. That's basically what my dad does full-time now—farms catfish in the two rivers crossing their property. The pub will be crowded, but I'll save you a seat at the bar."

"That sounds like fun. I'll be there."

At the B and B, he walked her to the door. Someone had left the porch light on. Neither being in its glare nor Colleen's claim to be exhausted deterred them from a lengthy, romantic goodbye.

Colleen tiptoed upstairs after unpacking the basket in the kitchen and leaving Kendra a quick note of thanks. As she climbed into bed, Colleen looked forward to the next evening with a joy that had eluded her far too long.

THE NEXT MORNING Colleen helped Kendra prepare rooms for three sets of new guests. "I've been talking nonstop," she finally said. "I knew you'd want to hear about my memory coming back, and what the doctors said."

"I'm so happy for you, Jo…er, Colleen. I can't tell you how much I'll miss having you here with us, but I understand you need more to live on than Jim and I can afford to pay you. Hey, there was an ad in yesterday's paper for a job you could do. The Gatlinburg Visitors' Center is looking for greeters. There are no fee stations for traveling in the Smoky Mountains like there are in the other parks. Visitors generally stop at one of three centers near the entrances to pick up maps, brochures and park rules. The greeters are there to hand out the information and answer any questions."

"Wouldn't that be a part-time job? Seasonal, anyway."

"Not according to the ad. The park is open year-round. You should go over there right now and apply."

"I believe I will. If nothing else it will be a good lesson in interviewing."

"They'd be fools not to hire you with your looks and your smile."

"Yeah, right. They'll probably look at me and think Little Orphan Annie. Anyway, I'm sure they'll have tons of applicants."

"None with your poise. I guess that's one thing to thank your mother for. She may have done some terrible things, but she gave you that."

"Thanks, Kendra. I do need to remember that she wasn't all bad."

"Bad enough. Now go put on that sundress you wore the other day. I'll draw you a map to the Visitors' Center."

An hour later, Colleen couldn't believe her good luck. After she filled out the lengthy application and had a half-hour interview with the center's director and assistant director, she walked out employed. She and the other greeter would work rotating five-day shifts to cover the full week. The pay was better than she expected.

Colleen spent another hour in Gatlinburg rounding out her wardrobe, then rushed back to Buttercup Cottage. She had barely enough time to celebrate with Kendra and Jim before she needed to change and meet Garret at the pub.

She hoped he'd be excited for her. He ought to be. It meant she'd be staying in White Oak Valley.

It took a good ten minutes to find space to park. The pub's lot was full. Garret hadn't been kidding about the popularity of catfish Tuesday.

She'd taken care to use eye makeup and put on a foundation to cover some of the freckles that came out in droves in the summer. Confident she looked her best, Colleen slipped in through the heavy oak door. She was briefly stuck behind a group of big men who chatted and drank beer, probably awaiting a table, which seemed all to be taken. Easing her way through them, Colleen could see the bar where Sean and Garret worked side by side serving customers. One woman stood out. A voluptuous brunette in a low-cut dress who wore a seductive smile as she leaned over the bar. She ran one manicured finger down Garret's shirtfront. He refilled the woman's beer glass and, to Colleen, appeared to be laughing only inches from Jaclyn Richmond's pouty red lips.

Three of the guys who had blocked Colleen's way moved on to a recently cleared table and left Colleen with an unobstructed sightline.

More people came in as Garret picked up two empty

mugs and spotted Colleen. He waved her over to join
him at the bar. But she'd already turned to leave, giving
him a view of her rapidly retreating jade T-shirt and
bobbing red ponytail.

Garret's heart stuttered. He jerked back from
Jaclyn so fast he almost lost a shirt button. He
ducked under the hinged section of the bar, calling
Colleen's name loudly even before he reached the
closing door.

His sister-in-law Sheila, who sat at a table with Trish
Collier, left her seat. "Whoa, boy," she said, grabbing
Garret's arm and stopping him in his tracks.

Trish rose and joined Sheila. "Garret, stop acting
like a fool. What will your customers say about how
you just treated Jackie?"

"Let go. You don't know the whole story. Jackie
dumped me a week ago. You should go talk to my
parents. I spent this morning explaining what Sharon
Drake did to Colleen. Yesterday she remembered her
accident and a lot of other parts of her past. Mom's
going to invite Colleen to design pottery again. And
Molly's planning to see if she'll help weave baskets."
Shaking himself loose, he skirted the crowd at the door
and ran out of the pub. Looking around, he spotted
Colleen half a block away. He shouted for her.

His longer legs let him catch up to her quickly, and
they reached her car at the same time. She turned to
him impatiently. "You don't need to explain that
touching scene at the bar, Garret. I get it."

"If you get it," he said, breathing hard from his mad dash, "why did you run away?"

"I know you two were together, Garret."

"Not really."

"I've never had a problem with my eyes. I know what I saw. She was playing with your shirt, and you were laughing."

"Jaclyn is a born flirt. We had a casual friendship and she ended it. She's already moved on," he said, sticking to his agreement with Jackie.

"She told me she expected you to propose by the end of the arts and crafts fair."

Closing his eyes, he heaved a sigh. "Trish and Sheila cooked that up. It got out of hand. Come back to the pub with me and I'll have Jackie tell you everything."

"You can't do that. How humiliating for her."

"That's another reason I love you, Colleen. You care about other people's feelings. Please come back. You saw how busy we are. I left Sean and Brian to handle one of our busiest nights. And the folks are working the kitchen. I talked to them today, Colleen. They know what you've been through. Just come back for a while, okay? I want all of White Oak Valley to see we're a couple again."

"All right. I have some news, too. I got a job as a greeter at the Gatlinburg Visitors' Center. The salary's not great, but it's enough for me to live on."

"It's fantastic if it keeps you in town." Garret held out his hand and was relieved when she took it.

Back at the bar, he commandeered an empty seat. Jackie had gone back to sit with Trish and Sheila.

The first thing Garret did was pour Colleen a sarsaparilla that he delivered with a passionate kiss. Catcalls went up from the customers around the bar.

Over the course of the busy night, a number of longtime residents drifted over to formally welcome Colleen home. Molly waited tables. She stopped once to give her a supportive hug.

By eleven, the only people still in the pub were those involved in cleanup, and Sheila, Trish and Jackie.

Colleen began making excuses to leave. When his dad summoned him to the kitchen, Garret instructed Colleen not to take off.

Once he was gone, Jaclyn left her table and crossed the pub to speak to Colleen. "There's something I need to say while I'm slightly buzzed. In high school everyone knew Garret was in love with you. After Jake and I split, Trish and Sheila talked me into trying to cheer the poor guy up. I knew it was hopeless because he started too many sentences with 'Colleen and I used to do'…this or that or the other thing. I know his family wanted things to work out between us, but he was never able to forget you. Let me just say you're a lucky woman. Very few of us will ever know what it's like to be loved like that."

A lump in her throat stopped Colleen from replying, which was probably just as well. With a toss of her hair, Jaclyn turned and strolled back to her friends. She picked up her purse, and the three women left the pub.

Molly emerged from the kitchen's swinging doors in time to see Jackie leave Colleen and walk out with her friends. "Colleen, I don't know what Jackie said to you, but those three have always been tight. I was there today when Garret told our parents about all you've been through. I'm really happy you've come home. I know you need time to adjust, but I meant to tell you the other day, I haven't enjoyed the Mountain Music Festival since you left. It's in two weeks. If you and Garret go, I thought my husband, Matt, and I might join you. I'd like you to meet my family. Matt's in a band that sometimes plays at Logan's. He plucks a mean mandolin. I hope one day you'll be comfortable enough to join them occasionally. They play old bluegrass tunes like 'Buffalo Gals,' 'Mountain Dew,' 'Snowflake Reel' and 'Foggy Mountain Breakdown,' to name a few."

Colleen smiled. "'Foggy Mountain Breakdown' sounds like what I suffered, Molly. I'd love to go to the music festival, but Garret and I haven't discussed it."

"What haven't we discussed?" he asked, coming out of the kitchen.

Molly told him, and he said, "I'll be happy for us to go together. I didn't talk about the festival, Colleen, because I was afraid it would bother you if you couldn't remember it."

"I wouldn't even be here if it wasn't for those music awards and the high-school yearbooks. I'm ready to embrace everything about the life I had here, Garret."

"Then come back to the kitchen and say hello to my folks. I told them I'd ask, but couldn't guarantee you'd agree."

He lifted the hinged portion of the bar and as she went through, Colleen murmured, "You know something? This feels like old times, and I love it."

CHAPTER ELEVEN

DONOVAN LOGAN was a burly man with dark hair and hazel eyes. Colleen used to be a little intimidated by him because he bellowed at his sons, but Molly always declared him a teddy bear. Now the gentle hug he gave Colleen, the soft way he said, "Welcome home, love," had her blinking away tears.

She couldn't see that Clare Logan had changed a bit in seven years. The blond, blue-eyed dynamo looked up from scrubbing the grill. "Colleen, I'm so glad you've finally found your way back to us. I truly believe that things turn out best for people who are willing to work at it. I'd hug you, but my hands are soapy."

"I'm glad I'm here, too. I'm also relieved to know where the random phrases that crept into my thoughts while I was gone came from. They were yours. Garret called them 'momisms.' One I clung to five or so years back was 'the three essentials of happiness are something to do, someone to love and something to hope for.'"

It was Clare's turn to wipe tears from her eyes. She

pressed her cheek to Colleen's. "Give the girl a scrubby," was all she said. Then she turned to Garret. "The kitchen floor still needs mopping. Get with the program, son. Remember, the family that works and prays together, stays together."

"Listen to you giving orders? Do I need to remind you that you and Dad sold the pub to Brian, Sean and me?"

"All the more reason you shouldn't have to be told what to do to close."

Snickering, Colleen found a scrubby and plunged it in the soapy water.

"Don't you two be ganging up on me," Garret warned as he pretended to bite her neck.

Nevertheless, it was only after a stern look from her that he filled the water bucket and picked up the mop.

At the very end of the night, Donovan pried tops off several bottles of beer and passed them around to his sons. "Can't beat 'em, guys. No use trying." He saluted the women with his bottle. Brian and Sean, who'd just come in the back door carrying empty garbage cans, arched eyebrows as they put the cans away and took the beers. Sean said, "I don't even have to ask what we missed. We ran into Trish, Sheila and Jackie in the parking lot. They told us enough for us to get the picture. We apologize for trying to run you off, Colleen."

"You didn't know. I didn't know the whole truth myself until yesterday. All is forgiven." Smiling, she turned back to cleaning her portion of the grill.

And that was pretty much how she was absorbed back into the Logan family, she decided later when Garret walked her to her car.

"I didn't take you into the back room to turn you into kitchen help." Picking up both her hands, he kissed her reddened palms.

She squeezed his fingers. "I really felt accepted. And I'm finally in charge of my own destiny. There won't be anyone hovering around telling me what's bad for a virtuoso's fingertips. I can clean and scrub and mess with clay and basket bark all I want."

"If it's cleaning you're looking for, Colleen, feel free to come to my house and dig in."

"I think I'm ready to see your house, Garret. I need to find a place to live, but other than playing at the B and B, I have no set plans until I start work next Monday."

"Come tomorrow morning. I'll fix you breakfast."

"Let me take care of breakfast. All I need is directions." Garret gave them to her, then took her in his arms.

A horn honked before he could do much more than that. Brian rolled down the window of his pickup and yelled, "Hey, no smoochin' on a public street, little brother." His cackle was cut off by Sean, who joined in with his brotherly advice.

Garret reluctantly released Colleen. He took her keys and opened her door. "Mom and Dad will be by next. It's going to be harder than I imagined to let you go every night. Sean and Trish have been engaged six months and I don't know how he manages. So, promise me you won't sign a long-term lease."

Colleen thought about his words as she drove back to Buttercup Cottage. And as she lay alone in bed. Despite sharing an apartment with her mother for so long, Colleen felt she'd lived a solitary life. She didn't want to anymore.

That thought stayed with her through the night and into the morning even as she picked up ingredients to fix Garret buckwheat pancakes for breakfast. She knew how much he liked them.

The directions Garret had given her made finding his home easy. The road leading to it wound through beautiful old-growth trees, but the house itself sat on top of a hill that had been cleared. Colleen hadn't expected to recognize anything, but seeing it stirred memories. Constructed of wood and local stone, the house offered a warm, welcoming facade. The main section was two stories high, with single-story extensions on either side. She recalled arguing with Garret over her insistence they line the porch with hanging baskets of flowers and potted greenery. She was deeply touched to see that he'd fulfilled that wish of hers even though she hadn't been around.

Garret must've been watching for her. He flung open the front door, Domino dancing around his legs. "What took you so long? I phoned to see if you were still at the B and B. Kendra said you left forty minutes ago."

Colleen held up two grocery sacks she hauled out of the backseat. "I promised you breakfast, silly. You think I wiggled my nose, and bacon, eggs and buckwheat appeared?"

"Buckwheat? Did you ask Mom what I like best?"

"I remembered you'd have eaten buckwheat cakes every morning if your mother had fixed them."

It wasn't until Colleen reached the porch that she saw he was barefoot and still unshaven. She was about to tell him how sexy he looked, but he grabbed her around the waist and delivered a good-morning kiss that took her breath away. She lost her grip on one bag, and when she heard it hit, she didn't even care if it was the one with the eggs. She was sure they could find other ways to fill their time if breakfast was ruined.

"Mmm," she sighed as Garret let her stand on her own again. "For a greeting like that I could learn to like to cook every morning."

"I was afraid you'd gotten lost in the hills. I was giving you five more minutes and then I was going out searching."

"I can follow directions, Garret. Oh, good, it was the flour and milk I dropped." Bending, she patted Domino's head and reached for the bag, but Garret relieved her of both sacks.

"What do you think of the house?"

She stroked his stubble and savored the rough feel of it on her fingertips. "I love the outside. Elements of the design came back the minute I drove up. It was sweet of you to hang fuchsias."

He stood aside to let her walk in first, and even held Domino back. "I drove Dad and my brothers crazy insisting we incorporate every last detail of your design. Except furniture," he mumbled. "We never talked about how we would furnish the house. That's probably why I only have the bare essentials. Now that you're here, we can buy what you want."

Looking around, Colleen saw he hadn't been kidding about the interior being bare. The living room boasted a leather couch, a floor lamp and a portable bar. A fitting bachelor pad, she supposed. However, the gleaming cherrywood floors were just as she had imagined and didn't need much ornamentation. A set of heavy forest-green curtains stood open, and sun made the room warm and inviting.

From there, Garret led her into the kitchen. Neutral ceramic floors matched cherry cabinets. The counter was granite with a glass-tile backsplash.

Colleen removed her light jacket and hung it over a chair. "This is beautiful."

"Let's finish the tour, then I'll help you fix breakfast."

Downstairs there was a master bedroom suite and an office/den. Three unfurnished bedrooms and two full baths were upstairs. Each bedroom had a view of the hazy valley. None of the rooms had been lived in.

"Why did we want a house with so many bedrooms?" Colleen asked as once again the dog escorted them down the wide stairs. "I've honestly forgotten."

Garret pulled her to him, and kissed her with feeling. "We were going to fill them with babies. Our babies," he said in a husky voice.

Colleen was transfixed by his smoldering eyes. "Oh, Garret, I'm sorry. I remember at the waterfall the day before you went on your trip, you predicted our babies would all have my red hair. I said okay, as long as they had your dark eyes. But then I lost our first."

"Hush. That was a long time ago. The doctor said you could have more. We're young enough yet to have several. If we get busy," he added with a wink.

Colleen didn't think he was teasing. "I'm so grateful we have a second chance. When I leave here today I'm going to ship Jerrold's violin back to him. Have I thanked you yet for turning around that day? Otherwise, Jerrold would've forced me to go back to Boston, and we wouldn't be here now." She shivered as they returned to the kitchen.

Garret rubbed her arms warm. "I said I wouldn't rush you, but it's not easy," he said as he got out the mixing bowls. "I'll try harder if you promise you'll tell me when the time is right. Otherwise I'll bug you every day about setting a firm wedding date."

She held out her pinkie finger, and he curled his around it, just as they'd always done when they were kids dashing in and out of each other's houses. Now, touching foreheads, they dissolved in laughter. "Can you believe we did that?" she exclaimed, shaking her head.

"I can. We both had to grow up fast, sweetheart. Too fast. I think we deserve to play a little now."

As Colleen mixed the pancake batter, Garret scrambled the eggs and put the bacon in the microwave. "I can't believe I never doubted Mother's stories, that I never questioned my lack of friends. She said I attended private schools and stressed that all my free time was spent with music tutors. I was so stupid to let her make my decisions for me, Garret."

"You couldn't have done anything differently. She was all you had," he said, moving the eggs around the pan.

Colleen flipped the pancakes, which were turning golden brown. "I remember how angry she was the day I announced I'd seen a Help Wanted sign in the window of the coffeehouse near our apartment. She had a fit after I admitted I'd filled out an application and would be working an evening shift the next day. Now it's so easy to see why she objected. I served couples my age. I envied them, and that was the beginning of my dissatisfaction with my life of practice, performances and more practice."

Garret passed her two plates and she added pancakes to the bacon and eggs he'd already served up. "It's a wonder to me that you can stand to pick up a violin," he said.

They sat at the kitchen table. Garret broke off a

piece of one pancake and gave it to Domino while he waited for Colleen to finish with the butter.

"You shouldn't feed a dog under the table. Sorry, it's your dog and your table," she said, looking shame-faced.

"It's just been us here at mealtimes since he showed up on my porch half-starved. I held him on my lap and coaxed him to eat for weeks. He was so skinny he could barely keep his head up. The vet said he may have been poisoned."

"Oh, my goodness! He's lucky he picked your porch."

Garret shrugged, and they went on to talk about more trivial matters. But the story of how Garret saved the hound lingered in Colleen's mind. Last night, Jaclyn Richmond said Garret loved her the way few women were ever loved. He was a good man. Now, in her quest for independence, she was holding him at arm's length. Was this really the freedom she was looking for?

She debated that question the rest of the day. She boxed Jerrold's expensive violin, insured it for a small fortune and sent it on its way.

She assured herself she'd make Garret a better wife if she felt she wasn't missing out on experiences most people her age would've had.

He seemed content enough. Colleen noticed that, the next morning when she phoned him to ask a favor. "Garret, say no if it's an imposition, but since I'm going to be working at the Visitors' Center, I think I ought to be able to describe the highlights of Smoky Mountain Park firsthand. Would you give me the grand tour?"

"Do you have anywhere specific in mind?"

"I'd hoped you might suggest the most sought-after spots."

"The park is so big we won't be able to make much of a dent between now and when you start work on Monday. Cade's Cove and Cataloochee are historic sites. Do you remember how to ride a bike?" he asked, clearly warming to the idea. "I haven't biked the loop since I left the Boy Scouts. My parents still have a couple of bikes, if you're game."

"I seem to recall that we used to bike all over town. I'm in."

"We'll see how you do tomorrow, city girl. If you're still standing at the end of the loop, we'll borrow horses from Galen and ride back in to Mingus Mill on Friday. I can catch you up then on the other museums and places visitors will want to see."

Colleen offered to provide lunches both days.

"Lunch is no problem, Colleen," Kendra said later. "Maybe we ought to run down to the sport fishing store and pick up a couple of backpacks. And those insulated water bottles with the spout you can drink from while you ride."

"I wouldn't have thought of any of that. How did you get so smart?"

"Well, I wasn't cloistered like you were."

At the store, the salesman asked if the women were hiking alone.

"No," Colleen volunteered. "Why? Are these places dangerous?"

"There have been a few reported black bear sightings lately. You should be okay. They've been out of hibernation a couple of weeks, and berries and fruit are beginning to pop out. Just keep in mind that mama bears are under a lot of pressure to find food for their cubs, and they can be quite irritable. Even a bear that seems to lumber can move astonishingly fast."

"Maybe we should skip packing a lunch," Colleen said worriedly.

"That's the other thing I was about to mention. This pack with the thin metallic lining will allow you to store leftovers if you stop to eat someplace without ranger-approved waste cans. Those are the metal kind with lock-on tops."

"Okay, I'll take two of these. Garret has lived here all his life. I don't think he'd suggest showing me areas where we need to worry about bears."

The women paid for their purchases and returned to the B and B.

"I wish you and Jim could go with us," Colleen said. It was easy to see that Jim Rowan felt bad about not being able to go on the fun outing, though he did his best to hide it. "Babe, you should go along," he urged Kendra. More longingly he said, "The clinic doctor said that when I get fitted for prostheses, I'll be able to ride a bike. Then we can do it again together."

"Colleen only bought two of the bear-proof back-packs, Jim. Besides, you know as well as I do that the lodging business is a twenty-four/seven deal."

Colleen purposely glanced away as she zipped up the last pack. She wanted to give Kendra and Jim privacy to share a lingering kiss. Still, she was shaken by the depth of Kendra's commitment to her husband.

Garret noticed her unusual quietness when he picked her up. "Are you worried that this will be too much for you? I checked with Dad. He said it's an eleven-mile loop—an easy ride even for a novice."

"I'm not worried about the ride. I just witnessed Kendra's complete selfless love for Jim. Life has been so difficult for them, and I was wondering how anyone can be that certain their feelings for another person will survive."

"You're getting too philosophical for me."

"So you don't know, either?"

"Love is what it is," he asserted. But he shoved a CD into the Vitara's player, and whistled along to "Night Train to Memphis."

Did that mean he couldn't swear he loved her that much? Or was he afraid to hear her doubts? Colleen brooded all the way to Cade's Cove. She came to the conclusion that she didn't really know what to expect of love. Or perhaps she hadn't paid attention. She knew that her parents' marriage hadn't been all that loving, but Garret's folks seemed happy.

He broke into her thoughts. "This is where we'll start our ride," he said, stopping the Suzuki. All that time to get here wasted and Colleen still hadn't put her confused feelings for Garret into words.

They'd inadvertently chosen the right day for their trip. The loop was closed to traffic and there were only a few hikers and other bicyclists. They saw grouse running through the brush and an elk feeding in a lush green field.

"The man at the fishing store said there are a lot of black bears this year. I don't know whether to hope we see one or not."

"Our chances will be better when we get into the trees. Are you doing okay? Am I pushing you too fast?"

"I'm enjoying this. In Boston I sometimes went days without getting outside except to go from the car to the conservatory. I hope my legs still work tomorrow."

"You'll have to let me know if you're all right for riding horses tomorrow. I told Galen we may need to borrow his rig to truck the horses up to the Cataloochee."

"I didn't think to ask if they're tame enough for a beginner. I rode bikes when we were kids, but I never rode horses, did I?"

"Your mom wouldn't allow it. She was sure you'd get bucked off and break an arm. Galen lived at home then, so we didn't have that access. We had to rent, and it wasn't easy to come up with the fee."

"I'd like to try. I want to try a lot of things I've never done before."

"You mean like rock climbing, hang gliding or parachuting?"

"Well, maybe not those things precisely." She glanced at him with amusement.

"We're about halfway, Colleen. It's still early, but I suggest we take a break and eat our lunch. Is down by that brook all right? I wish I'd thought to bring fishing poles. Or at least some line to tie onto willow branches."

"It's just as well. Would you really want to carry fish six miles back to your car in our backpacks?"

"You never used to be squeamish."

"I think you said I used to be a tomboy. I guess I'm more of a girly girl now."

"Yeah. No complaints from me." He nuzzled her neck as they walked their bikes down to the brook. Lunch got put on hold until they heard voices up on the road and hastily rearranged each other's T-shirts.

They found a log to sit on and Garret had their lunches unpacked when the other bikers rounded the hairpin curve.

"Phew, that was a close call," Colleen said, blushing.

"I should know better than to start something we can't finish. What do you say we skip lunch and go back to my place for a nooner?"

"Okay. Race you back," she said, surprising and delighting him.

They almost couldn't get back to his house quickly enough. By the time they got inside Garret's front door, they were already pulling at each other's clothes.

Domino charged them, happy to have company so early. "Damn," Garret muttered. "I'll meet you in the bedroom. I've got to put the dog in the laundry room with a rawhide bone or we won't have a minute's peace." He threw the last over his bare shoulder as he coaxed Domino down the hall.

Colleen was worried they'd lost momentum, but it didn't take long to build the passion again after Garret returned. More memories of the many times they'd snuck away to make out as teenagers flooded her in the throes of their lovemaking. "That was a lot like parachuting," she murmured as he collapsed on top of her. "Do you realize this is the first time we've ever made love in a bed?"

"I hope there'll be many more. Colleen, sweetheart, I know I promised not to push you to the altar. But explain to me why we need to wait when we've already waited way too long. I want to go to sleep with you every night and wake up with you beside me in the morning. Every night and morning until we're older than dirt." He rose over her, his eyes more serious than she'd ever seen them. He tenderly stroked her hair, still damp from their lovemaking.

She didn't get a chance to answer because her cell phone rang. She shot up out of bed. "Who would be calling me?" she asked as Garret fumbled to extract her phone from her jeans. "No one calls me but you." She took it with shaking hands. "Maybe it's a wrong number."

When she answered, she found it was for her after all. It was her new boss at the Visitors' Center. "No, no. I can start tomorrow. It's no trouble. I'll be there at eight sharp." Her eyes sought Garret's as she hung up.

He'd already crawled off the bed and was collecting his clothes. "That takes care of our horseback ride."

"I'm sorry. Someone quit unexpectedly. I have to get home and read up on the park attractions."

He passed her her clothing. Nothing more was said about marriage. Instead, she waited in the Vitara while he put the bikes in his garage and let Domino out of the laundry room.

OVER THE FOLLOWING WEEKS, Colleen and Garret saw little of each other. With more summer vacationers in the area, her work and his got busier. She came home beat every afternoon. So beat she hadn't taken time to look for any possible rentals. It was easier to stay at the B and B. She still helped Kendra with the housekeeping, and continued to play for their guests on weekends. She experimented with less classical pieces and played more traditional and bluegrass songs that she discovered she liked.

She and Garret talked to each other on the phone late at night. Mostly about how their workdays went, and less about personal stuff. "This is frustrating," he told her one evening. "I want to see you. Hold you. The family asks about you. Molly's the only one you've seen. She said you and she are doing some baskets."

"Yes, she's teaching me again. I love it. I wish I had more time."

"Have you told Kendra you need the Saturday off for the music festival?"

"Yikes, that's coming up fast. I will, Garret. I promise. We were going to be there all day, and then back to the pub for a wind-down party?"

"That's right." He yawned in her ear, forcing them to say good night.

A few days after that, Colleen rolled in late from work. She noticed Kendra bustling around, dashing upstairs with clean bedding.

"Hold on, let me help," Colleen called. "I didn't think there were any new guests until the weekend."

"Jim's folks are coming," Kendra said as Colleen joined her in one of the rooms. "Actually, Colleen, they're coming to stay. Jim's dad retired. And we have news," she said, fussing with knickknacks on the antique dresser. "I went to the doctor today. I'm pregnant. Colleen, I'm so excited. But, practically speaking, Jim and I can't manage the B and B and care for a baby."

Colleen knew she shouldn't be surprised. Kendra's shining eyes attested to the depth of her happiness. "I'm delighted for you both." Rounding the mattress she'd been fitting a sheet to, she hugged her friend.

"Have you done anything about finding a place to live?" Kendra looked worried. "The last thing I want to do is boot you out. But with Jim's parents taking up one of our bigger rooms, we can't have as many guests. And because you've been helping out so much, we reduced your rent. A baby will be an added expense. Oh, Colleen, we want you to take your time. Stay until you can find a place that works for you."

The Rowans' good news meant that Colleen had to reevaluate her comfortable existence. She'd slipped into a rut, she thought as she lay in bed that night. She'd moved through her days without looking ahead.

She probably shouldn't take time to attend the music festival. That was a whole Saturday where she should dig in to locate an apartment.

But none of these was the real reason she felt unsettled. It had been Kendra's surprising disclosure. Colleen laced her hands across her scarred stomach. She'd wanted her and Garret's baby so much. She'd embraced the idea of motherhood even at eighteen. To make the home she lacked. Garret knew she wanted a garden; he'd promised to till one for her.

Here at Kendra's she picked vegetables from the garden, cleaned and cared for their house, when the truth was she wanted a home of her own. She wanted a family of her own. She wanted Garret, but she'd been afraid to admit it. Because she'd been promised those things once, and they'd all been taken away.

GARRET KNEW when he came to pick Colleen up for the music festival on Saturday that something was different. Wrong. "Is work going okay?"

"It's fine." She shrugged. "You drove past Molly's. Aren't she and Matt and the kids riding with us?"

"Nope. Casey woke up in the night with itchy spots. They don't know if it's hives or chicken pox. If it turns out to be hives from the strawberries the kids ate yesterday, Molly and Matt will meet us at Logan's tonight for the party."

"Why didn't you call me? We could have skipped going today."

"Are you kidding me? You've looked forward to this for weeks."

"I know, but..." She stared down at her hands.

"What's the matter?"

"Kendra's pregnant," she blurted.

Garret grinned. "That's wonderful. Wait, is there a problem with her, with her, ah, condition?" He shifted in his seat, a little embarrassed.

"No. She's fine. Glowing in fact." Tipping her head back against the headrest, Colleen gazed listlessly out her window, watching the scenery.

Garret didn't press further.

The musicfest was in full swing when they arrived. Most of the contestants, performers and judges had rolled in well in advance. Many of them were friends who met year after year.

Garret parked the Suzuki between a Dodge Ram van with a gun rack in the back window and a small pickup with a top-heavy camper.

Stepping out first, Garret waved. "The Silvermans are in the next row unloading their instruments. Would you like your fiddle? I have it in the backseat. The one you used to play at the pub."

"I'm not entered, and I'm really, really rusty."

"Kendra said you… Well, maybe you'll get fired up. Listen, the holler is jumping."

It certainly was. Unable to hold back, Colleen began to tap her fingers and toes in time to the twangy sound rising from small stages all around the park. She couldn't believe how many old-timers recognized her. Several sidled up to talk. Two or three had instruments her father had carved. One banjo player, as wrinkled as the tree bark, said gruffly, "Sorry to hear about your daddy. He bragged a lot about you being the most gifted fiddler to ever hit Tennessee. That's the God's truth. Gal, you've grown purty as a painting. Keep on having fun with your music."

"Who is that?" Colleen whispered to Garret once the old man had moved on.

"Marty Young. He's played with Flatt and Scruggs. Marty helps head up MerleFest now—you know, the music festival in memory of Merle Watson."

They wandered around from stage to stage, listening to the contestants.

A quartet from North Carolina embraced Colleen as one of their own. After much cajoling, they managed to talk her into joining them onstage for "Tom Dooley," "Casey Jones," and a rocking rendition of "Tom Cat Blues." Her bow flew over the strings, and her smile lit up her face.

Garret leaned against a tree trunk, watching her play, love and pride shining from his eyes.

Colleen stumbled in a round robin where each musician played faster and faster. When it was over, the audience applauded her all the same, Garret loudest of all. Still, she bowed out when the next tune, "Mama Don't Allow," was called out.

Out of breath but still beaming, Colleen pulled Garret's head down for a kiss. "There was too much my mama didn't allow for me to want to play that song," she admitted.

The afternoon ended too soon. Garret hated to drag Colleen away. "I'm due at the pub at six o'clock." He tapped his watch.

"All right, let's go. I had so much fun. How can I thank you enough for bringing me?"

He could think of a few ways, but kept them to himself. Rather, he helped her into the vehicle and set her fiddle case in her lap.

Colleen babbled excitedly as they drove down the mountain and into town. When they pulled up in front of the pub, she started to set her case in the backseat, but Garret stopped her.

"Bring it in," he said. "Half of White Oak Valley will be drifting in to party tonight. You used to play here for weddings, wakes and just because. Nothing would please me more than to see you continue on where you left off at the musicfest."

"Just me, you mean? I don't know if I can play blue-grass solo."

"Old Jerrold thought you were good enough to solo in Europe. I can tell you this will be a much easier crowd."

"Okay, then. For you," she said quietly. She slid her arm through his, and they entered the already-crowded pub as a couple.

Clare, Molly and Garret's sisters-in-law were traips-ing from the kitchen to the main bar room, serving bowls of thick beef stew.

Garret's mom was first to notice them. She saw the fiddle case, too. "Matt's been telling everyone you were going to entertain us tonight, Colleen. My favorite is 'Flying In The Wind.' Will you play it for me tonight?"

Colleen hadn't said she remembered the tune, but Garret boosted her onto the stage where Matt and two younger guys were banging out "Cotton-Eyed Joe." Colleen drew her bow across her violin, and soon the trio played backup in softer tones. The crowd whistled and stamped their feet each time her quivering bow dropped to her side.

During a particularly energetic solo, Garret vaulted onto the stage behind her, swept her hair aside and planted a kiss on her neck.

There was a roar of appreciation from the men close to the bar. All lifted frosty mugs of Tennessee ale in a toast.

Grinning from ear to ear, Colleen didn't miss a beat. Tilting her head back, she aimed a kiss at his lips. She might have faltered when he grabbed her waist and deepened the kiss. Or when she leaned closer to yell in his ear, "This is my kind of music, Garret. I know it now. This is my town. And you're my man."

Garret signaled to Matt to take over the song. The three men in the band moved to the front of the stage and kicked up the pace of "My Dixie Darling." Garret lifted Colleen down.

"Did you mean that, Colleen?"

"Yes. While I played 'East Tennessee Blues,' it hit me why I thought your neon sign was wrong the day I arrived. You wanted to buy the pub by yourself. I was going to entertain. Our sign was going to read Garret and Colleen's Irish Pub."

"That's right. We planned to double our parties and wedding receptions."

The musicians broke for refreshments. Some thoughtful patron started plugging quarters into the jukebox.

The crowd that was grouped around the stage moved back and helped clear space for dancing. Garret twirled Colleen out for the first dance.

She pressed close to him, basking in his possessive touch. "What would you say if I suggested the next wedding reception in the pub be ours?" she murmured.

"If you mean that, it would make me the happiest man alive."

"I mean it with all my heart. Call me a slow learner. Today every time I looked up and saw your smile, I couldn't imagine living without you again. You've made me feel complete, as if the missing pieces of my life have finally come together."

He spun her off the floor and into a dark corner where he poured his love and his answer into one long kiss that promised a lifetime of wedded bliss to follow.

* * * * *

The Colton family is back!
Enjoy a sneak preview of
COLTON'S SECRET SERVICE by Marie Ferrarella,
part of THE COLTONS: FAMILY FIRST
miniseries.

Available from Silhouette Romantic Suspense in
September 2008.

He cautioned himself to be leery. He was human and he'd been conned before. But never by anyone nearly so attractive. Never by anyone he'd felt so attracted to.

In her defense, Nick supposed that Georgie could actually be telling him the truth. That she was a victim in all this. He had his people back in California checking her out, to make sure she was who she said she was and had, as she claimed, not even been near a computer but on the road these last few months that the threats had been made.

In the meantime, he was doing his own checking out. Up close and exceedingly personal. So personal he could feel his blood stirring.

It had been a long time since he'd thought of himself as anything other than a law enforcement agent of one type or other. But Georgeann Grady made him remember that beneath the oaths he had taken and his devotion to duty, there beat the heart of a man.

A man who'd been far too long without the touch of a woman.

He watched as the light from the fireplace caressed

the outline of Georgie's small, trim, jean-clad body as she moved about the rustic living room that could have easily come off the set of a Hollywood Western. Except that it was genuine.

As genuine as she claimed to be?

Something inside of him hoped so.

He wasn't supposed to be taking sides. His only interest in being here was to guarantee Senator Joe Colton's safety as the latter continued to make his bid for the presidency. Everything else was supposed to be secondary, but, Nick had to silently admit, that was just a wee bit hard to remember right now.

Earlier, before she'd put her precocious handful of a daughter to bed, Georgie had fed his appetite by whipping up some kind of a delicious concoction out of the vegetables she'd pulled from her garden. Vegetables that, by all rights, should have been withered and dried. She'd mentioned that a friend came by on occasion to weed and tend it. Still, it surprised him that somehow she'd managed to make something mouthwatering out of it.

Almost as mouthwatering as she looked to him right at this moment.

Again, he was reminded of the appetite that hadn't been fed, hadn't been satisfied.

And wasn't going to be, Nick sternly told himself. At least not now. Maybe later, when things took on a more definite shape and all the questions in his head were answered to his satisfaction, there would be time to explore this feeling. This woman. But not now.

Damn it.

"Sorry about the lack of light," Georgie said, breaking into his train of thought as she turned around to face him. If she noticed the way he was looking at her, she gave no indication. "But I don't see a point in paying for electricity if I'm not going to be here. Besides, Emmie really enjoys camping out. She likes roughing it."

"And you?" Nick asked, moving closer to her, so close that a whisper would have trouble fitting in. "What do you like?"

The very breath stopped in Georgie's throat as she looked up at him.

"I think you've got a fair shot of guessing that one," she told him softly.

* * * * *

Be sure to look for COLTON'S SECRET SERVICE and the other following titles from THE COLTONS: FAMILY FIRST *miniseries:*
RANCHER'S REDEMPTION by Beth Cornelison
THE SHERIFF'S AMNESIAC BRIDE by Linda Conrad
SOLDIER'S SECRET CHILD by Caridad Piñeiro
BABY'S WATCH by Justine Davis
A HERO OF HER OWN by Carla Cassidy

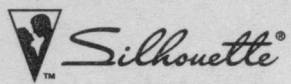

Romantic
SUSPENSE

Sparked by Danger, Fueled by Passion.

The Coltons Are Back!

Marie Ferrarella
Colton's Secret Service

The Coltons: Family First

On a mission to protect a senator, Secret Service agent Nick Sheffield tracks down a threatening message only to discover Georgie Gradie Colton, a rodeo-riding single mom, who insists on her innocence. Nick is instantly taken with the feisty redhead, but vows not to let his feelings interfere with his mission. Now he must figure out if this woman is conning him or if he can trust her and the passion they share....

Available September wherever books are sold.

**Look for upcoming Colton titles
from Silhouette Romantic Suspense:**

RANCHER'S REDEMPTION by Beth Cornelison, Available October
THE SHERIFF'S AMNESIAC BRIDE by Linda Conrad, Available November
SOLDIER'S SECRET CHILD by Caridad Piñeiro, Available December
BABY'S WATCH by Justine Davis, Available January 2009
A HERO OF HER OWN by Carla Cassidy, Available February 2009

Visit Silhouette Books at www.eHarlequin.com SRS27598

SAVE $1.00

A riveting trilogy from
BRENDA NOVAK

SAVE $1.00

on the purchase price of one book in The Last Stand trilogy from Brenda Novak.

Offer valid from May 27, 2008, to August 30, 2008.
Redeemable at participating retail outlets. Limit one coupon per purchase.

52608328

5 65373 00076 2 (8100)0 11499

MBNTRI08CPN

REQUEST YOUR FREE BOOKS!
2 FREE NOVELS PLUS 2 FREE GIFTS!

HARLEQUIN®

Super Romance®

Exciting, emotional, unexpected!

YES! Please send me 2 FREE Harlequin Superromance® novels and my 2 FREE gifts (gifts are worth about $10). After receiving them, if I don't wish to receive any more books, I can return the shipping statement marked "cancel." If I don't cancel, I will receive 6 brand-new novels every month and be billed just $4.69 per book in the U.S. or $5.24 per book in Canada, plus 25¢ shipping and handling per book and applicable taxes, if any*. That's a savings of close to 15% off the cover price! I understand that accepting the 2 free books and gifts places me under no obligation to buy anything. I can always return a shipment and cancel at any time. Even if I never buy another book from Harlequin, the two free books and gifts are mine to keep forever.

135 HDN EEX7 336 HDN EEYK

Name	(PLEASE PRINT)	
Address		Apt. #
City	State/Prov.	Zip/Postal Code

Signature (if under 18, a parent or guardian must sign)

Mail to the Harlequin Reader Service:
IN U.S.A.: P.O. Box 1867, Buffalo, NY 14240-1867
IN CANADA: P.O. Box 609, Fort Erie, Ontario L2A 5X3

Not valid to current subscribers of Harlequin Superromance books.

Want to try two free books from another line?
Call 1-800-873-8635 or visit www.morefreebooks.com.

* Terms and prices subject to change without notice. N.Y. residents add applicable sales tax. Canadian residents will be charged applicable provincial taxes and GST. Offer not valid in Quebec. This offer is limited to one order per household. All orders subject to approval. Credit or debit balances in a customer's account(s) may be offset by any other outstanding balance owed by or to the customer. Please allow 4 to 6 weeks for delivery. Offer available while quantities last.

Your Privacy: Harlequin is committed to protecting your privacy. Our Privacy Policy is available online at www.eHarlequin.com or upon request from the Reader Service. From time to time we make our lists of customers available to reputable third parties who may have a product or service of interest to you. If you would prefer we not share your name and address, please check here. ☐

HSR08R

#1 *New York Times* Bestselling Author

DEBBIE MACOMBER

Dear Reader,

I have something to confide in you. I think my husband, Dave, might be having an affair. I found an earring in his pocket, and it's not mine.

You see, he's a pastor. And a good man. I can't believe he's guilty of anything, but why won't he tell me where he's been when he comes home so late?

Reader, I'd love to hear what you think. So come on in and join me for a cup of tea.

Emily Flemming

8 Sandpiper Way

"Those who enjoy good-spirited, gossipy writing will be hooked."
—*Publishers Weekly* on
6 Rainier Drive

On sale August 26, 2008!

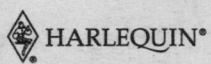

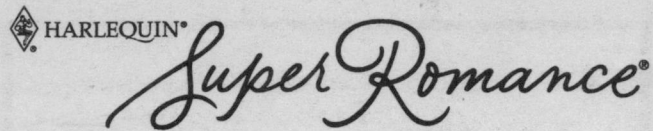

COMING NEXT MONTH